I0591842

The Puzzle With The Piazza

by Mark Dunn

∥SAMUEL FRENCH∥

MUSIC AND THIRD-PARTY MATERIALS USE NOTE

Licensees are solely responsible for obtaining formal written permission from copyright owners to use copyrighted music and/or other copyrighted third-party materials (e.g., artworks, logos) in the performance of this play and are strongly cautioned to do so. If no such permission is obtained by the licensee, then the licensee must use only original music and materials that the licensee owns and controls. Licensees are solely responsible and liable for clearances of all third-party copyrighted materials, including without limitation music, and shall indemnify the copyright owners of the play(s) and their licensing agent, Concord Theatricals Corp., against any costs, expenses, losses and liabilities arising from the use of such copyrighted third-party materials by licensees. For music, please contact the appropriate music licensing authority in your territory for the rights to any incidental music.

IMPORTANT BILLING AND CREDIT REQUIREMENTS

If you have obtained performance rights to this title, please refer to your licensing agreement for important billing and credit requirements.

THE PUZZLE WITH THE PIAZZA opened at South City Theatre in Irondale, Alabama on October 22, 2020. The director was Donna Stinson Williamson. The stage manager and lighting designer was Sharon Morgan. The sound engineer and photographer was Steven Ross. Set design was by Donna Williamson and Donald Norwood. The poster design was by Delaine Derry Green. The videographer was Brooke Dennis. The cast, in order of appearance, was as follows:

ALTHEA WITLIN..........................Dianna Brown Murphree
LEIF MORRELL.....................................Tom Robinson
MATTIE PLESHETTE .... Katy Walker
CONNIE MORRELL................................ Victoria Smith
INA GLUCK.....................................Sally Montgomery
RADIO VOICES ....Todd Ponder, Sharon Morgan, Mike Gerrells

CHARACTERS

in order of appearance

ALTHEA WITLIN – mid to late seventies
LEIF MORRELL – thirty-three
MATTIE PLESHETTE – mid-twenties to early thirties
CONNIE MORRELL – thirty-one
INA GLUCK – early to mid-seventies
and the pre-recorded radio voices of one woman and two men.

SETTING

Except for brief interludes presented in limbo, the play is set in Althea Witlin's basement "rec" room. Althea lives in an unnamed mid-sized city in the American Midsouth.

TIME

The play is set at the turn of the century. (The most recent one.)

AUTHOR'S NOTES

The dramatic engine of *The Puzzle with the Piazza* is the working of a large jigsaw puzzle. It isn't necessary – and, moreover, it would be logistically problematic – to present to the audience an actual puzzle at its various stages of assembly. The author recommends, therefore, that the table be elevated or angled in such a way that the audience won't be able to closely monitor the mechanics of assembly. Instead, progress is gauged from indication: character movement, gesture, and dialogue. To be clear, the characters won't be *pantomiming* putting a puzzle together; they will actually be moving real puzzle pieces around in service to verisimilitude, but the staging should give the audience the freedom to employ their own imaginations in terms of how this task is proceeding. And there is a dividend in this manner of staging: an enhancement of those moments of poetic revelation, which transcend the nuts-and-bolts reality of connecting the pieces themselves.

THE PUZZLE WITH THE PIAZZA
DESCRIPTION

The year is 2000, the place: the basement rec room of septuagenarian Althea Witlin. Althea's life is about to change in a very big way. Health issues are forcing her to give up her house and move in with her sister Ina across town. Perhaps just as important: the move requires Althea to give up all of her jigsaw puzzles. Yet there is this one puzzle, described by her new friend Leif Morrell as "the mother of all jigsaw puzzles," which she's never had the gumption to tackle. Together, Althea and Leif decide to defy the odds and try to finish this puzzle in the hours that remain before Althea must go. They are joined by next-door neighbor Mattie, learning to be newly independent after years in a group home, and by Leif's wife Connie, who has come face-to-face with the realization that she and Leif can't be biological parents. Together all four members of Althea's "puzzle platoon" push personal challenges and problems to the side as they place gondolas upon the canals of Venice and pigeons into the bright blue sky above the piazza. The play is a bittersweet comedy about tenuous family ties and the often stronger bonds of friendship that lattice and enrich the final years of our lives.

The Puzzle with the Piazza *is dedicated to the many theater groups around the U.S. and Canada who worked heroically to keep theater alive during the dark days of the pandemic by streaming live book-in-hand performances to thousands of quarantined audience members.*

And especially to those dozen theaters that chose the story of Althea and her friends to share with their audiences. Together we put all those Venetian pigeons into the sky!

ACT ONE

(Lights come up on a basement "rec" room. Prominent in the center of the room is an old and dusty ping pong table, its net mouse-nibbled to tatters. Otherwise, the room displays the usual recreation room furniture and paraphernalia, including a mirrored ersatz Gay Nineties-looking bar with counter and four rickety stools, and a bar cabinet, laced with cobwebs. An old tabletop radio sits on the counter. Open shelving in a different cabinet on the other side of the room is crammed with stacks of jigsaw puzzle boxes. There is also a folding chair somewhere in the room. We hear footsteps descending an offstage staircase. The room's only visible door is opened by ALTHEA WITLIN. She and LEIF MORRELL step into the room. She looks about, smiling as memories sally forth.)

LEIF. So, when *was* the last time you came down here?

ALTHEA. Oh goodness. I can't even remember. That terrible storm last spring, I think. I was worried about the possibility of flooding.

LEIF. And was there – ?

ALTHEA. *(Shaking her head.)* Dry as a bone. My neighbors weren't so fortunate. Oh, the things you can learn from nature's fury: cat boxes float. Snooker tables do *not*.

LEIF. *(Looking about.)* The room: it looks entombed.

ALTHEA. Is that a good assessment, dear, or a bad one?

LEIF. Just an observation.

ALTHEA. This was my son's rec room. Well, it was my husband's to begin with, but Collin took it over. He was mad about ping pong. Oh, he hated it when I called it ping pong. "It's table, tennis, Mother. Show some respect!" He was very good. He won the city teen championship two years in a row.

LEIF. *(Leaning against the table.)* Where is he now?

ALTHEA. Collin lives in San Diego. I get cards. Watch the dust there.

LEIF. I could turn this into a home office.

ALTHEA. Oh, you don't want an office down here. There aren't any windows. You should put your office upstairs in the little room off the landing. It has a southern exposure. You can sit and feel the warmth of the morning sun right there at your desk.

LEIF. That room just might have to be a nursery.

ALTHEA. Oh, you have a baby!

LEIF. Not yet. We're expecting.

ALTHEA. How far along is she, dear?

LEIF. *(Adding it up.)* About twenty hours past the home pregnancy test. Connie was gonna take another one this afternoon just to be sure.

ALTHEA. A baby. That's so nice.

LEIF. We've been trying for five years.

ALTHEA. Oh dear, a lot of people would have given up by now.

LEIF. Connie wants a baby come hell or high water. Well, I do too. You were really kind to show me around – I mean, without the real estate agent.

ALTHEA. Oh, wasn't she brash? I was so glad when she left. She told me not to mention any of the house's shortcomings. Well, great goodness, every house has shortcomings. An honest seller makes for a happy buyer, I always say.

LEIF. I should probably be getting home.

ALTHEA. It was so nice to meet you.

LEIF. I'll bring Connie on the weekend if you're gonna be around.

ALTHEA. I'm afraid I'll be gone by then, dear. In fact, my sister – Ina – she's coming to pick me up tomorrow. Ina and all those movers: it's going to be bedlam around here.

LEIF. You're moving in with your sister?

ALTHEA. Yes. Which means most of this stuff is going right into storage. I'll just be getting the one room. It used to be her sewing room. It will feel like a closet. I'm not complaining. The room has a southern exposure. But it was a challenge, believe me: deciding what to take, what not to take. I know now what a trial it must be for the ones of us who end up in the nursing homes: having to pare down from a lifetime's worth of possessions to what will fit into two or three suitcases.

LEIF. You don't seem all that happy to be moving.

ALTHEA. Well, I'm *not*, dear, but I don't have much choice in the matter. I shouldn't be living alone. My health has betrayed me with a vengeance.

LEIF. I'm sorry to hear that.

ALTHEA. *(Shrugging it off.)* What do you do, dear? For a living. If you told me, I'm afraid I've forgotten.

LEIF. I work for WZPG. In the advertising department.

ALTHEA. Oh, I'm always listening to that station. Mostly late at night. It's a strange assortment of people who call those shows. They have *theories*.

LEIF. *Theories*: that's a kind way to put it.

ALTHEA. And then you've got your insomniacs. And there are those who listen just for the company, I think.

    (**LEIF** *nods.*)

The voices can be a comfort. The quiet – that late night quiet: after all this time I still haven't gotten used to it.

LEIF. I'm not sure I could get used to it either.

ALTHEA. Well, you go on home to your wife. Do you like the house?

LEIF. It's a very nice house.

ALTHEA. You can say it's not for you. I won't mind, really. Some people object to the bay window.

LEIF. The bay window is a nice feature.

ALTHEA. Some say it looks – what was it that one fellow called it? – "*imposed.*" He said my bay window looked imposed. He preferred one more "organic."

LEIF. I'm not quite sure what— [that means]

ALTHEA. I think it means he didn't like the house. But someone will come along who will appreciate it. Someone who likes a house with a certain "lived in" quality. Don't you get that feeling? That "lived in" feeling? It's like buying pre-washed jeans, isn't it?

LEIF. *(Smiling.)* You could say that.

    (*Indicating the "puzzles" cabinet.*)

Your family liked jigsaw puzzles.

ALTHEA. Oh, it was a weekend ritual. For a time. Then Reed – that was my husband – Reed and Collin – well, they just got too busy. Places to go. People to see. Jigsaw puzzles take time, you know. Time and infinite patience.

    (**LEIF** *gravitates toward the puzzle cabinet.*)

LEIF. I have the patience. Never have the time, though.

ALTHEA. Places to go. People to see. I believe a person has to *make* the time.

LEIF. *(Poking around.)* A *lot* of time judging from the number of pieces in some of these boxes.

ALTHEA. I kept working the puzzles for a while after my husband and son stopped. But it wasn't the same. Jigsaw puzzles can be enjoyable solitary endeavors, but I prefer to approach them more communally, if you know what I mean.

LEIF. Here's one with two-thousand pieces!

ALTHEA. *(Correcting him with a gentle shake of the head.)* One-thousand-nine-hundred-and-ninety-nine. Reed considered suing the manufacturer. To have come so far, it was beyond cruel.

LEIF. *(Inventorying the other boxes.)* Two-thousand. Twenty-five hundred.

ALTHEA. Open the doors at the bottom.

LEIF. What's in there?

ALTHEA. You'll see.

> **(LEIF** *opens the cabinet doors as instructed. His hands fall on a large box.)*

LEIF. *(Examining it.)* Three-thousand. This must be a record.

ALTHEA. You just might be right.

LEIF. *(Pulling it out.)* Three-thousand pieces. Just where would you work a puzzle this big?

ALTHEA. It actually fits right here. On this ping pong table.

LEIF. You've worked it before? But the box doesn't look like it's ever been opened.

ALTHEA. I took measurements.

LEIF. And then you changed your mind.

ALTHEA. *(Smiling.)* I did. I chickened out. A three-thousand-piece puzzle is quite intimidating. But it's a pretty picture, don't you think? The Grand Canal in Venice. Isn't it beautiful?

LEIF. I like the colors. I like puzzles with lots of colors.

ALTHEA. Open it up.

LEIF. I'm really tempted.

> (**ALTHEA** *encourages him with a nod. He gets the lid off the box.*)

ALTHEA. Did you work puzzles when you were a child?

LEIF. Off and on. I was an ambivalent puzzle worker.

ALTHEA. Why do you say that?

LEIF. Well, I liked the feeling of accomplishment that came when all the pieces got put together, but there was also a certain, you know, *letdown.*

ALTHEA. That it was over.

LEIF. Right – and the fact that the final product was really kind of – I don't know – kind of *impractical.* It wasn't something you could use, you know?

ALTHEA. Well, you could *look* at it, couldn't you? You could take a – a – take an aesthetic view of the thing.

LEIF. Like, hmm, like a piece of art you put together.

ALTHEA. You've got it!

LEIF. But the "getting there" – that was fun too. Like the way looking *forward* to Christmas always kind of felt better than Christmas itself.

ALTHEA. So, you enjoyed the communal aspect of puzzle-working yourself.

LEIF. I guess I did. The mindless banter. Yeah, I liked that.

> (**LEIF** *takes a lingering look inside the box. He whistles his astonishment.*)

ALTHEA. *(Grinning.)* Are we intimidated?

LEIF. *(With good-natured bravado.) Nothing* intimidates *me*, Ms. Witlin.

ALTHEA. Please call me Althea.

LEIF. All right.

ALTHEA. And you're Leif. Like the Viking.

> (**LEIF** *nods, smiles.* **ALTHEA** *peers inside the box.*)

You know, I just might be tempted to give it a try after you've gone. It will be my last chance. Ina's always hated jigsaw puzzles. Ever since we were kids. She'd hide the pieces and make things difficult.

> *(A beat.)*

We were never close.

LEIF. *(Confused.)* But you're going to live with her.

ALTHEA. She's mellowed with the years.

> *(Beat.)*

I hope. Pour it out on the table.

> (**ALTHEA** *removes the net from the table so* **LEIF** *can dump the pieces right into the middle. Note: if any of the pieces fall through the gap, incorporate the business of picking up the escaped pieces through the following exchange.*)

The mice and the silverfish have been kind to this puzzle. You should see the Renoir over there: the little girl with the watering can. You put the puzzle together and discover that silverfish have sucked up part of that sweet little girl's face.

LEIF. I should call Connie and tell her I'll be a little late.

> *(He takes out his cell phone and punches in a number.)*

You shouldn't have to turn all these pieces over by yourself.

ALTHEA. Yes, that part is so tedious.

LEIF. *(Glaring at his phone.)* I'm an idiot.

ALTHEA. What's that, dear?

LEIF. I forgot that Connie doesn't have her cell anymore. She thinks she left it in the dressing room at the Fashion Barn.

ALTHEA. Would you like something to drink?

LEIF. That lemonade you gave me earlier – that was really good.

ALTHEA. It *was* good, wasn't it?

> **(ALTHEA** *exits.* **LEIF** *punches in another number.)*

LEIF. *(Into cell phone.)* Hi pumpkin. I'm guessing you're still at Beth's. I'm also guessing you won't listen to the answering machine when you get home. I know how much you hate answering machines. But just in case you do, I wanted to let you know I'll be a little late. I'm over at Ms. Witlin's. You know the house I told you I was gonna look at on my way home? You really should see it. I think you'd like it. Anyway, I shouldn't be too late. There's just something I need to do before I head home. See you later, "Maw."

> *(He chuckles to himself, hangs up and digs into the puzzle. Lights fade out and come up*

on **ALTHEA**, *who stands in limbo downstage under a pin spot. She holds glasses of pink lemonade, one in each hand, and speaks directly to the audience.)*

ALTHEA. With a puzzle of this size, it's crucial for one to develop a very focused strategy. You simply *have* to have a strategy or you'll be fumbling around for hours without making any progress at all. Now, mine isn't unique. Maybe you do this yourself. You isolate all the straight-edge pieces. You put all the others aside so you can work your border first. You have to finish your border to get your bearings. Then you work inward from the border, moving methodically toward the middle, expanding your pockets of color. Now, I know there are other ways to approach a jigsaw puzzle, but this one has always worked for me: creating a frame, a nice frame for your picture. Pictures need frames, don't you think?

(In a conspiratorial whisper.)

I have to get back to the basement. You see, I don't have much time. Ina is coming for me tomorrow afternoon.

(She leaves the spot and returns to the basement where lights come back up. **LEIF** *is working away. Note: from here until the end of the play, when characters are stationed at the ping pong table they will – unless directed otherwise – be working on the puzzle. The dialogue, though quite often about everything but the puzzle itself, will very rarely pull them from the fundamental task of completing their collaborative enterprise.)*

(Continued, handing **LEIF** *one of the glasses of lemonade.)* Did you reach your wife, dear?

LEIF. Thank you. No. She's probably still at her sister's. We need better light. That bulb's pretty dim.

ALTHEA. There might be brighter ones in the little cabinet behind the bar. If they're still good. It's been years since Reed bought them.

> (**LEIF** *goes to the bar and pulls out a dusty box of bulbs. Over the next minute or so he will take the bulbs out, one by one, and shake them next to his ear to determine if the filament is still intact.* **ALTHEA** *goes to the table and continues to turn over the puzzle pieces.)*

I always wanted to go to Venice. Wanted to sit right there in Saint Mark's Square and sip that hardy Italian coffee and breathe in all the scents of that beautiful ancient city.

LEIF. I hear it smells like mold and mildew.

ALTHEA. Oh, I hope not. Goodness, look at this.

LEIF. What?

ALTHEA. There was a hair in that box.

LEIF. Let me see.

ALTHEA. *(Holding up the hair.)* Look how long it is. It, no doubt, belonged to a woman. Probably the very woman who packed the box.

LEIF. You don't think that was done by a machine?

ALTHEA. Well, maybe she was the woman who *ran* the machine. Oh Lord! What if she got her long hair all tangled up in that machine?

LEIF. I'm sure they have ways of extricating people's hair from machines.

ALTHEA. *(Distressed.)* Oh, it might have *scalped* her!

LEIF. We won't think about that.

> (**ALTHEA** *disposes of the hair. She laughs to herself.)*

What is it?

ALTHEA. I was thinking about Reed. My late husband. I do that, now and then: imagine how he might respond to some of the silly observations I find myself making these days.

LEIF. You mean like the hair thing?

ALTHEA. *(Nodding.)* Of course, I would never have brought up such a thing with Reed. He had no patience for, for *trivialities.*

(She laughs. Then, in her husband's voice.)

Althea. Do you really think this, this *discovery* of yours makes any difference in the universal scheme of things?

(Returning to her own voice.)

"Universal scheme of things." That was his favorite phrase. I don't know what it means. Leif, do you know what that phrase means: "Universal scheme of things"?

LEIF. Let me think about this.

(He thinks it over.)

I think it means the grand, lofty design for the universe.

ALTHEA. And whose design would that be?

LEIF. God's, I guess. I mean, if you believe in God.

ALTHEA. No, I don't think that's what Reed meant.

*(**LEIF** crosses to **ALTHEA** with one of the bulbs in hand.)*

I think he simply meant that I should change the subject. Is that a good bulb?

LEIF. I'll try it.

(Indicating the folding chair.)

Can I use this chair?

ALTHEA. Be my guest. I don't think silverfish eat chair metal.

> (**LEIF** *gets the chair and proceeds to unscrew the hanging light bulb. Once the connection is broken, the whole room (and stage) goes black.*)

LEIF'S VOICE. That was dumb.

ALTHEA'S VOICE. Hold on. I think I know where the flashlight is.

> (*We hear the sounds of* **ALTHEA** *bumping around in the dark, then the darkness is sliced by the beam of a flashlight. She aims it at* **LEIF,** *who is still standing on the chair.*)

ALTHEA. (*Addressing, we assume, the batteries inside the flashlight.*) Thank you, Energizer Bunny!

> (**LEIF** *puts in the new bulb. It works; the room is bathed in light.*)

LEIF. *Voila!*

> (*He hops down from the chair.*)

Better?

ALTHEA. Oh, *much* better!

> (*She puts away the flashlight.* **LEIF** *disposes of the old bulb.*)

LEIF. What would your husband have thought of this brand-new century?

ALTHEA. Oh, he would have hated it.

LEIF. Why do you say that?

ALTHEA. Well, he hated living in the *twentieth* century, and this new one doesn't seem to be any different. I think he had hopes that people in the new millennium would be less silly. But we aren't, are we?

*(**LEIF** smiles in agreement. **ALTHEA** picks up the box and looks at the picture on the top.)*

Every time I think about Venice, I picture Katharine Hepburn in that movie where she falls into the canal. She got a bad eye infection or something from that.

LEIF. Katharine Hepburn or the character she played?

ALTHEA. *Katharine* got the infection. I don't believe the *character* she played had any eye problems at all. Which is good. Otherwise, it would have changed the whole story. I recall that it was a love story. She was in love with Rossano Brazzi. Oh, wouldn't that have been sad? They fall in love, and the woman gets an eye infection and she spends the rest of the picture with this big gauzy bandage over one eye?

LEIF. That might be a little distracting.

*(He joins **ALTHEA** at the table.)*

ALTHEA. I might be mistaken, but I think Katharine Hepburn got sick when she went to Africa to do that movie, *The African Queen*. Do you know that picture?

LEIF. *(Nodding.)* My mother loved Katharine Hepburn, so growing up I saw pretty much all of the old Katharine Hepburn movies.

ALTHEA. Seems like she was always going off on location and coming down with something. But it's had no effect on her longevity, has it?

LEIF. How old is she?

ALTHEA. Well into her nineties, I think. They did a story on her in *People*. She swims every morning in her lake.

LEIF. She trembles a lot.

ALTHEA. It's probably because the water's cold.

LEIF. Are you *sure* this puzzle is gonna fit on this table?

ALTHEA. Well, if I've miscalculated, we'll just have to find ourselves a bigger surface. But I believe it will. You'll see.

> *(She just realizes something.)*

Oh.

LEIF. What?

ALTHEA. Well, you've got to go, don't you? After you turn over the pieces.

LEIF. Says who? Now, how much fun would *that* be? Flipping all these puzzle pieces and then just heading for the door.

ALTHEA. Well, I'd certainly be happy to have your help, however long you wanted to stay.

> *(Something strikes her.)*

Oh. What about your wife?

LEIF. *(Not a concern.)* Connie gets with Beth and the two of them talk for hours. I'll probably still beat her home.

> *(Now something strikes him.)*

You don't need to be doing any last-minute packing or anything like that, do you?

ALTHEA. I've already packed the things I'm taking to Ina's. The movers are supposed to box up everything else. Eventually, Ina's going to help me do a big garage sale. Have you ever been to Venice? Have I asked you that already?

LEIF. Never been to Venice. Didn't travel much growing up. And now – well, Connie's afraid of flying.

ALTHEA. I heard someone say once that no one is afraid of *flying*. It's *crashing* they're afraid of.

LEIF. *(Smiling.)* I guess you're right about that. How long has it been since your husband passed away?

ALTHEA. Oh, I'd have to count it up. But he wasn't my husband when he died. Reed and I divorced and then a few months later he died. That's good because the reverse would be difficult, don't you think?

LEIF. I suppose it would.

ALTHEA. We were married for twenty-two years: some of them happy, others not so happy. We came to the conclusion – quite early in the marriage – that we were quite incompatible. But by then I'd had Collin, and since the marriage wasn't all *that* fractious, we just decided to stick it out until our son grew up, and that was probably for the best.

(Pointing to a spot on the table.)

You missed that little pile there.

LEIF. Thanks.

ALTHEA. Although it's never a picnic being married to someone who doesn't love you.

LEIF. Did you –

(He hesitates.)

ALTHEA. Did I love *him*? Dear, you can ask me whatever you like. I don't keep secrets. Yes, I did love him. But then, Reed used to accuse me of loving *everybody*. I suppose that's my biggest failing. I find things about people – oh, even the most terrible sorts of people – I find things, little endearing things that keep me from disliking somebody *too* much.

LEIF. Even mass murderers?

ALTHEA. Well, mass murderers are usually insane, dear. They can't help themselves.

LEIF. So, you don't believe in evil?

ALTHEA. *(Considering this.)* I *suppose* I do. But even evil people aren't totally one hundred percent evil.

LEIF. What about Hitler?

ALTHEA. Well, this is an interesting conversation.

LEIF. I'm playing the, um, devil's advocate. I hope it's okay.

ALTHEA. I just don't recall ever having had such a conversation before.

LEIF. Not even with your husband? Or, you know, your son?

ALTHEA. Heavens, no! The three of us never discussed the nature of evil. It was hard enough just getting them to tell me what they wanted for dinner.

LEIF. I don't usually get all that philosophical myself.

ALTHEA. It's working this puzzle. It frees you up to *think*. To roam the countryside of your mind.

LEIF. That's a good way to put it.

ALTHEA. Thank you. And I think that Hitler was pure evil. He is my exception to the rule. I would not have him to dinner.

LEIF. You think about having famous people over to dinner?

ALTHEA. Oh, yes. I've been planning a special imaginary dinner party for years.

LEIF. Just famous people or a mix?

ALTHEA. Mostly famous people. And they must all be interesting conversationalists. I can't have anyone at my dinner party who isn't going to make some sort of contribution to the evening.

LEIF. Sounds like a plan. So how many people are on your guest list?

ALTHEA. It's up to twenty-seven. We'll all be seated at one very long banquet table.

LEIF. How many courses?

ALTHEA. Five sounds about right. Although one will just be cheese. I love cheese.

LEIF. *(Pointing to the table.)* There's a bunch right there.

ALTHEA. Thank you.

LEIF. So what—actors, artists, musicians...?

ALTHEA. Authors, scientists, politicians.

LEIF. Any presidents?

ALTHEA. I was tempted to invite several, but I didn't want the evening's conversation to lean *too* heavily toward the political.

LEIF. So, who did you choose?

ALTHEA. Theodore Roosevelt and Millard Fillmore.

LEIF. That's an odd pair.

ALTHEA. I wouldn't seat them together.

LEIF. Theodore Roosevelt is a good choice. I don't know anything about Millard Fillmore.

ALTHEA. That's exactly why I want to invite him. I don't know anything about him either. And I love his name. I would love to be able to say, "Could you pass the gravy boat, Millard?" "Fill it to the rim, Fillmore?"

(She giggles.)

LEIF. It sounds like it would be a fun dinner party. Are all of your guests dead?

ALTHEA. All but that little boy who won the national spelling bee last year. He seems like such a sweet, bright little boy. I thought he'd enjoy meeting all these illustrious historical figures. I still have three seats to fill. Would you like to come? I could put you next to Marie Antoinette. I can't wait to serve her dessert.

> (**LEIF** *gives* **ALTHEA** *a scrutinizing look. There is a joke there, but it's eluding him for the moment. His focus returns to the puzzle.*)

Look: the entire puzzle – now exposed!

That didn't take any time at all.

LEIF. Is Katharine Hepburn coming to your dinner party?

ALTHEA. Well, I hadn't thought about it. It might be fun to invite her. But I'd probably want to keep it a secret from the other guests.

LEIF. Why is that?

ALTHEA. *(Grinning mischievously.)* Oh, you just think about it.

LEIF. Okay.

> (*A doorbell rings, slightly muffled by the distance between the basement and the sound-box.*)

ALTHEA. Keep thinking about it. That's probably my paper boy. He was going to drop by to say goodbye.

> (**LEIF** *nods.* **ALTHEA** *exits.* **LEIF** *continues to work the puzzle for a moment, then stops, takes out his phone and punches in a number.*)

LEIF. *(Into phone.)* Beth, this is Leif. I was looking for Connie. I guess she told you about losing her cell phone. Sounds like the two of you are out on the deck. You know, I can't find a house with a deck half as nice as yours and Doug's.

(Snapping two pieces together, a tiny fanfare.)

Ta *dah!*

(Calling upstairs.)

The first official coupling, Althea!

(Into phone.)

Sooooo – when you get this message, tell Connie to call me. I need to find out what her plans are for the evening. Oh, and tell her I want to go to Venice. We can take a boat. We never did have a proper honeymoon, you know. See ya, sis.

(He hangs up. To himself, regarding the puzzle.)

That's one small step for man, one giant leap for Le Grand Canal of Venice. *Le* is French. What's Italian? Il Canal Grandatorri!

(He laughs to himself.)

I'm hungry. Mmm, cheese.

(He calls upstairs.)

Hey Althea, send that paper boy out for pizza!

*(A moment later, **ALTHEA** enters, accompanied by **MATTIE PLESHETTE**. **MATTIE** is special in ways that will soon be revealed.)*

ALTHEA. It wasn't the paper boy. It was my next-door neighbor Madeline Pleshette. She likes to be called Mattie, don't you, dear?

MATTIE. I was once called Maidenform. That's a bra.

LEIF. Nice to meet you, Mattie. I'm Leif.

MATTIE. Hello, it's nice to meet *you*, Leif.

ALTHEA. Mattie likes to work puzzles, don't you, Mattie?

MATTIE. I do. I do like to work puzzles.

> *(The two women move toward the puzzle and begin working on it, alongside* **LEIF.***)*

LEIF. *(To* **MATTIE.***)* Do you live in the big Tudor house or the other one with the arches?

MATTIE. I live in the one with the arches. Although I actually live in the room over the garage. It's semi-detached. That's what they say: it's a semi-attached garage with a room over it for Mattie. I have kitchen privileges. I only have a hot plate in my room. It is just one room. It doesn't have a kitchen. I keep my mayonnaise in the big kitchen in the house with the arches.

ALTHEA. *(To* **MATTIE.***)* Dear, what did I tell you about giving people more information than is necessary?

MATTIE. Oh, did I just do that?

ALTHEA. *(Nodding, gently.)* A person might prefer to hear such things sprinkled through a conversation as he gets to know you – not, perhaps, offered up all at once.

MATTIE. Oh yes. You're right.

LEIF. It's okay. I don't mind.

ALTHEA. I'm teaching Mattie social skills. Many things are new to her.

MATTIE. *(To* **ALTHEA.***)* Does this mean I have to wait to tell him about my cat?

ALTHEA. Why don't you ask him?

MATTIE. *(To* **LEIF.***)* I have a cat. Would you like to know some things about him?

LEIF. *(Now catching on that* **MATTIE** *is "different".)* Yes. I'm very interested in cats.

MATTIE. He's a stray. I picked him up the very day I moved into the garage room. I pulled him out of a dumpster over on McAdams Street. He was eating green bacon. He was very happy to come home with me. His name is Mr. Puss.

LEIF. *(Not judgmentally.)* That's an interesting name.

MATTIE. It was either going to be Miss Kitty if he was a boy, or Mr. Puss if he was a girl.

ALTHEA. Dear, I think you got that backwards.

(*To* LEIF.)

Mattie has only lived alone for a few weeks. But she's doing very well, aren't you, dear?

MATTIE. *(Proudly.)* I have steam heat.

ALTHEA. Mattie came over to give me a potholder she made in one of her classes. I asked her if she liked to work jigsaw puzzles.

MATTIE. *(To* LEIF.*)* I came over to give Althea a potholder which I made in arts and crafts, and she asked me if I liked to work jigsaw puzzles and I said yes-I-did, and she brought me down here to where you are.

ALTHEA. Honey, you're giving Leif too much information again. You were, in fact, repeating all the information I'd already given him.

MATTIE. I didn't need to do that, did I?

(*To* LEIF.)

Was your father's name "Tree"?

LEIF. *(Smiling.)* No. My name is spelled a little different from the kind of leaf you're thinking about.

MATTIE. Do you have a family tree? I hear that everyone has a family tree. Except me. I was raised by nuns.

LEIF. I'll bet you have a family tree. You just haven't been told what it is.

MATTIE. I hope it's a dogwood.

ALTHEA. Look at that! Mattie's been working this puzzle for only two minutes and she's already put three pieces together. Are you good at puzzles, dear?

MATTIE. Yes. I believe I am.

ALTHEA. That's wonderful. Can you stay for a while?

MATTIE. I was going to watch *Fashion Nine One One* at seven-thirty. But I can skip it tonight. And I have to feed Mr. Puss at eight. But that won't take too long. I love puzzles. I love to put them together and then I like to take them apart, piece by piece, and watch everything disappear.

ALTHEA. *(To* LEIF.*)* Mattie also memorizes square roots. She's memorized quite a few of them.

MATTIE. *(Nodding.)* I like numbers.

ALTHEA. *(To* LEIF.*)* I think she's a savant. I don't know if she meets *all* the requirements. But she's certainly a whiz at remembering square roots and she apparently has a facility for putting jigsaw puzzles together.

MATTIE. Look! There's a cute little girl on the plaza!

ALTHEA. You are a true asset, dear.

MATTIE. Thank you.

ALTHEA. Would you like some lemonade?

MATTIE. Yes. Put lots of sugar in it. I like a lot of sugar.

> (ALTHEA *goes out.* MATTIE *and* LEIF *work on in silence for a moment.)*

> *(Continued, pointing to her foot.)* I have a corn.

>> *(She goes to sit down and take off her shoe.)*

Are you going to buy this house? Althea said you might buy this house.

LEIF. I'm considering it. My wife hasn't seen it yet, though.

MATTIE. Oh, you have a wife. Is she nice?

LEIF. She's very nice.

MATTIE. This is a nice house. I sometimes sit at my window and look at it and wish that I lived here.

LEIF. Do you like the bay window?

MATTIE. Oh, yes. Althea says it's about as organic as a bay window can be. You know what that means? That means that you can put an organ in there and play it and open the window and everybody can hear the beautiful music. And you don't even have to be a nun.

(She holds up her now shoeless foot.)

Is this a corn? Or a callus? I can't tell the difference.

LEIF. *(Glancing over.)* I don't think I know either.

MATTIE. Corn is a vegetable. Like plum is a fruit. Mr. Puss picks up kibble with his paw. He eats like a raccoon.

(Putting her shoe back on.)

I have to get back to this puzzle. We have to finish it before Althea leaves.

(She returns to the table.)

I don't want Althea to leave.

LEIF. She's been a good friend to you, hasn't she?

MATTIE. *(Importantly.)* She's my best friend.

(Another silence as they work on.)

LEIF. *(A challenge.)* Square root of sixty-six.

MATTIE. Eight point one two four zero. I only take my square roots four places behind the decimal point. More than that, I think, would just be rude.

LEIF. I'll check it.

>   *(He goes to his briefcase and takes out a calculator.)*

Give it to me again.

MATTIE. The square root of sixty-six: eight point one two four zero.

LEIF. You're exactly right.

>   *(Beat.)*

You're very good.

MATTIE. I know. I like this room. It's very bright. I need more light in my room. There are too many trees around. I like trees, but it gets very dark. Am I giving you too much information?

LEIF. No. You're giving me just the right amount.

MATTIE. One of the nuns had a dog that peed in a toilet.

LEIF. That's amazing. Did he flush?

MATTIE. Of course, he flushed! It isn't good manners not to flush!

>   *(**LEIF**'s cell phone rings.)*

I'll get it!

LEIF. But it's *my* cell phone, Mattie.

>   *(**MATTIE** wiggles her fingers for **LEIF** to give her the phone.)*

Okay. Say, "Hello. You've reached Leif Morrell's cell phone."

MATTIE. I can do that.

(LEIF hands her the phone.)

LEIF. That button there.

MATTIE. *(Very formal.)* Hello. You have reached Leif Morrell's cell phone. May I help you? ... Mattie Pleshette... one moment please.

(She gives the phone to LEIF.)

It's a man named Doug.

LEIF. *(Nods politely, then into phone.)* Hi Doug... Thanks for letting me know. I'll give a call over there after they've had time to drive over. Do you have the number? Hang on.

(He looks about the room.)

I need something to – [write with]

(He glances at MATTIE.)

Mattie: remember this number.

(MATTIE nods.)

Five. Five. Five. Oh. Five. Four. Eight.

(Continued, into phone.) Thanks, guy.

(He disconnects. To MATTIE.)

Should I write it down?

MATTIE. Five. Five. Five. Oh. Five. Four. Eight. You don't have to write it down. Would you like to know the square root?

LEIF. You mean the square root of that phone number?

MATTIE. *(Nodding.)* It's two-thousand-three-hundred fifty-five point nine six zero one.

(LEIF *stares at* MATTIE.)

LEIF. It was just a phone number.

MATTIE. Every number has a square root. Even phone numbers. Althea's is one-thousand-nine-hundred-ninety-six point four one zero seven. Mine is one-thousand-nine-hundred-fourteen point six six seven three.

> (MATTIE *shrugs and smiles. It takes a moment for* LEIF *to collect himself after this.*)

LEIF. So, except for too many trees, you like your garage apartment?

MATTIE. *(Nodding.)* I have iris wallpaper in my bathroom.

LEIF. I'll bet it's pretty. Where did you live before?

MATTIE. The Calloway House. It's a group home. You live there in a group. The Calloway House has blue diamond curly-cue wallpaper in the living room and green-striped wallpaper in the bathroom.

> (*She wrinkles her nose pejoratively.*)

The address has a good square root, though: forty-four.

> (*The two work on in silence.*)

LEIF. Do you memorize *cube* roots?

MATTIE. I don't know what those are.

> (*The two keep working.* LEIF *smiles to himself.*)

LEIF. "Let us eat cake!"

MATTIE. What?

LEIF. Marie Antoinette. Dessert. "Let us eat cake!"

> (*He laughs.* MATTIE *laughs too, although it's apparent that she doesn't know why she's*

laughing. **ALTHEA** *enters with lemonade for*
MATTIE.*)*

ALTHEA. Guess who's coming to dinner?

LEIF. *(Smiling; now he gets it.)* Katharine Hepburn?

(**ALTHEA** *nods enthusiastically.)*

MATTIE. Can Katharine Hepburn also have cake?

ALTHEA. If she likes.

MATTIE. What about her daughter?

ALTHEA. Audrey isn't coming, dear. There isn't room for
two Hepburns at my dinner party.

(She hands the lemonade to **MATTIE,** *who
downs it thirstily.)*

I said goodbye to Devon. That's my paper boy. I caught
him coming up the drive when I went out to give the
hydrangeas a little drink. The real-estate woman said
she'll have someone water all the flowers, but I don't
trust her.

MATTIE. *I'll* water them.

ALTHEA. Would you, Mattie? That would put my mind at
ease.

MATTIE. *(To* **LEIF.**) Althea's sister has pretty flowers.

ALTHEA. Oodles.

(To **LEIF.**)

Ina is a master gardener. She grows competitive roses.

MATTIE. Will she let you work in her garden?

ALTHEA. She's going to give me a little plot. I'll grow sweet
peas and beefsteaks and try to keep out of her way.
She's very particular about her garden. Oh look, I'm
making progress on this gondola.

LEIF. We aren't working on the same gondola, are we?

ALTHEA. I don't think so. Let's check the box.

> (*She studies the picture on the top of the puzzle box.*)

There are several gondolas. Mine has two people. It looks like yours is carrying a whole family.

MATTIE. (*Without looking up; it's just a toss-in.*) I had a little doll family. But they couldn't swim. It was sad.

LEIF. (*To* **ALTHEA.**) My wife and her sister: they, um, just left for their aunt's house.

> (*Beat.*)

I'm not sure why.

ALTHEA. (*To* **LEIF.**) Maybe they wanted to give the aunt the good news.

LEIF. But Connie wasn't gonna tell anyone until after the second pregnancy test.

ALTHEA. If she's close to her sister and her aunt, I'm sure she'd want to tell both of them as soon as possible. You know: *maybe* she took the second test over at – what's her name: the sister?

LEIF. Beth.

ALTHEA. Maybe she took the second test over at Beth's house.

LEIF. That makes sense.

ALTHEA. We didn't have home pregnancy tests back when I was carrying Collin. We killed rabbits in those days.

MATTIE. (*Concerned.*) Killed rabbits?

ALTHEA. It's a figure of speech.

LEIF. (*To* **ALTHEA.**) Do you have grandchildren?

ALTHEA. Two little girls. Two little *angels*. I mean, from what I can tell from the pictures. And I have a Christmas video.

LEIF. You've never seen them in person?

(**ALTHEA** *shakes her head.*)

How old are they?

ALTHEA. Eight and, hmm, six, I think. Collin and Candy had them late. They weren't going to have children and then Candy changed her mind when she turned forty.

MATTIE. *(Automatically.)* Six point three two four five.

LEIF. *(To* **ALTHEA.***)* I don't understand why you haven't seen your grandchildren.

ALTHEA. Oh dear, it isn't a very happy story.

LEIF. Sorry. Didn't mean to pry.

ALTHEA. Now, I told you I don't keep secrets. My realtor – she doesn't like that. She doesn't want me to tell about the hot water heater.

LEIF. What's wrong with the hot water heater?

ALTHEA. It's old and leaks a little. It really should be replaced. Let's gather all the border pieces together, dear. It will be easier to find them that way.

LEIF. All right.

ALTHEA. Candy – Collin's wife – she says she's allergic to me.

MATTIE. Some people are allergic to candy. You can be allergic to *her*!

ALTHEA. She says I wear too much perfume.

MATTIE. I like your perfume. It smells like sweet peas.

LEIF. *(Sniffs, then to* **ALTHEA.***)* The scent is pretty, you know, *subtle*.

ALTHEA. I stopped wearing it altogether. To be accommodating. And I told them. "Hello, Collin dear. I just wanted you and Candy to know that your mother is now 'fragrance-free.'" And then I waited. The invitation for me to come out: well, it still never came.

LEIF. And he doesn't come here?

ALTHEA. *(Shaking her head.)* Collin hasn't been home since his father's funeral.

LEIF. That doesn't make a lot of sense.

ALTHEA. Well, here's the story; I'll put it in the tiniest peanut shell for you. When Collin was eighteen, I was going to drive him to the airport. He was supposed to participate in an invitational table tennis tournament. It was a very big tournament. If he won or placed well, it would significantly improve his national ranking. Well, I thought I'd go ahead and get the car out of the garage while he was finishing his packing. I thought he was still inside, you see. I didn't see him standing right there in the driveway.

MATTIE. She ran over his foot!

ALTHEA. That's right. I backed over my son's foot with the car.

MATTIE. She broke every bone. Even the one in his little toe.

ALTHEA. Mattie, dear, you're giving excessive information.

LEIF. *(To ALTHEA.)* You ran over his foot and he didn't go to the tournament?

ALTHEA. *(Shaking her head.)* Not to that tournament or to any other tournament. His promising table tennis career ended that very afternoon.

MATTIE. *(To ALTHEA.)* Can I tell how many operations he had?

(**ALTHEA** *nods reluctantly.*)

(*Continued, to* **LEIF**.) He had three operations.

ALTHEA. And still he walks with a little limp. At least he did when I saw him at his father's funeral.

LEIF. He never really let go of this, did he?

ALTHEA. (*Shaking her head.*) It was more than that, I'm afraid. Long before this happened, Collin somehow felt obligated to choose sides between his father and me. Take a guess whose he chose. Reed's been dead for years, and Collin still keeps me at a distance.

> (**LEIF** *nods. He exchanges a silent commiserating glance with* **MATTIE**.)

Please don't misunderstand me. My son is a good husband. He's a good father to his girls. He just doesn't want me for his mother. I have lived with this fact for so long that I've almost come to terms with it.

> (*She points to a place on the table.*)

There are some straight pieces over there.

LEIF. Thanks.

> (*He steps away from the table.*)

Is there a bathroom I can –?

ALTHEA. Of course, honey. The powder room off the front entrance hall. If you find suitcases blocking the door, just push them to the side.

> (**LEIF** *gives the puzzle a good looking-over before he leaves.*)

LEIF. I think we're making really good progress.

ALTHEA. (*A pleasant realization.*) We *are*, aren't we?

(As lights dim here, **LEIF** *leaves the table and walks downstage. A pin spot comes up on him as he stands with his back to the audience, facing upstage. We hear the sound of a toilet flush. Then he "zips up" and turns to address the audience. Perhaps he mimes washing and drying his hands as he speaks.)*

LEIF. What I find works best with a big puzzle like this is not going too long with any one particular strategy. It's better to be just a little scattershot, you know? Work on the border for a while, then shift to some really bright and colorful spot that won't be too hard to bring together. After that, move over to a large, single-color area and hone in on how the shape of the pieces fit together. To me, it kind of breaks up the monotony. Otherwise, it gets to be a pretty long slog. All you can see stretched out in front of you is hours and hours of puzzle-working. And that can be a little discouraging. So, I'd say go for those little triumphs like Mattie with that girl on the piazza. I guess she's got the little-girl strategy going. Hey, whatever works for you, right?

*(***LEIF*** *returns to the rec room as lights come up here.* **ALTHEA** *and* **MATTIE** *are dabbing at the table and at individual puzzle pieces with a stray cloth.)*

What happened?

ALTHEA. We had a little accident.

MATTIE. *(Embarrassed.)* I knocked over my lemonade.

ALTHEA. There was hardly anything left in the glass, sweetie.

MATTIE. The pieces are going to be sticky.

ALTHEA. It's going to be fine. We'll wet a couple of paper towels and every time our hand falls on a sticky piece we'll just give it a little wiping while we're thinking about it. Now hurry upstairs, dear, and get that roll of Bounty and run a few of the sections under the sink.

MATTIE. All right.

(Beat.)

I'm very sorry, Althea.

ALTHEA. Dear, you are making far too much out of it.

*(**MATTIE** exits. To **LEIF** after **MATTIE** has gone.)*

She's a dear girl, but she's so hard on herself. She's actually doing quite well on her own, but she views every little mishap as reason for why she shouldn't be living by herself.

LEIF. Does she *want* to be living by herself?

ALTHEA. She does. But she has doubts about her abilities. I try to build up her self-confidence as much as I can. Oh, your phone rang while you were in the bathroom. That's why Mattie knocked over her lemonade. She was going for your phone.

LEIF. *(Crossing to the bar.)* Did Mattie say who it was?

ALTHEA. Your wife.

LEIF. *(Looking at the phone.)* Is she calling back?

ALTHEA. No, dear. I think she told Mattie she was on her way over *here*. It looks like she's going to get to see the house after all. Isn't that nice?

(He pockets the phone.)

LEIF. I suppose so.

(He loses himself in thought.)

ALTHEA. Is anything wrong, dear?

LEIF. I'm not sure why she'd come over here.

ALTHEA. Well, it wasn't anything Mattie said. In fact, she didn't even mention the puzzle. Does your wife, Connie – does she like jigsaw puzzles?

LEIF. *(Still preoccupied.)* I don't know. I mean I – well, I don't remember us ever working one together.

ALTHEA. Do you think she'd like to help us?

LEIF. *(Probably not the best of ideas.)* We'll probably need to go once she gets here. Your house is on the way home from her aunt's. I'll bet that's why she decided to drop by.

(**LEIF** *is back to working on the puzzle.*)

ALTHEA. I'd like to meet her. I'll bet she's an angel.

LEIF. *(A glimmer of a smile.)* She's pretty special.

(**MATTIE** *enters with a whole roll of paper towels, dripping wet.*)

ALTHEA. *(To* **MATTIE.***)* Dear, you wet the whole roll.

MATTIE. It fell in the sink.

ALTHEA. *(Pointing to the bar.)* Put it over there. We'll peel off a few pieces.

(**LEIF** *holds up a puzzle piece.*)

LEIF. This one's sticky.

MATTIE. *(Exuberantly.)* I'm on the job! I'm on the job!

(**MATTIE** *takes a wet paper towel and goes to* **LEIF***'s aid. She diligently scrubs the piece and hands it back to* **LEIF.***)*

LEIF. Thank you.

MATTIE. *(Indicating the piece.)* That goes in the window in that big bubbly-top cathedral.

LEIF. Which window?

MATTIE. *(Pointing.)* The one right there.

ALTHEA. Mattie, damp-wipe those pieces right there and then get back to work on the puzzle. Your puzzle-working skills are just as important as your custodial ones. Oh dear, my hands are very sticky and gummy.

> (**ALTHEA** *goes to the wet paper towel roll and runs her fingers up and down it.* **LEIF** *is still holding the puzzle piece. He doesn't put it down. He stares ahead, deep in thought.* **MATTIE** *stops what she is doing to study him.* **ALTHEA** *is doing the same.* **MATTIE** *seems to be working herself up to say something... which she finally does.)*

MATTIE. *(To* **LEIF,** *importantly.)* There's no baby.

LEIF. *(Shaken out of his reverie.)* What?

MATTIE. Your wife. She thought she was going to have a baby, but she's not.

ALTHEA. Mattie, honey, how on earth would you know this?

MATTIE. I heard the lady talking. The lady who was with her.

ALTHEA. What did the lady say?

MATTIE. She said, "Don't tell him you're not pregnant until you see him." She was crying.

ALTHEA. Who was crying, dear?

MATTIE. Leif's wife.

> *(This hits* **LEIF** *hard.* **MATTIE** *goes to him. She seems to want to do something demonstrative to comfort him, but she's apparently out of her element. She ends up giving tiny pats to his shoulder.)*

My mother only had one child. Me. This is what the nuns told me. My mother had a little baby and she dropped her on her head and then she left the little baby at the orphanage.

ALTHEA. The nuns didn't tell you any such thing, Mattie!

MATTIE. Yes, they did. They said my mother accidentally dropped me on my head when I was nine months old. Three.

ALTHEA. Which is it, dear? Were you nine months old or three months old?

LEIF. *(Absently.)* She was nine months old. Three is the square root.

MATTIE. They said I wore a tiny baby-doll neck brace for four months. Square root: two. I didn't know they made neck braces for dolls, did you?

ALTHEA. Mattie, I think maybe someone wasn't telling you the truth.

MATTIE. Yes, they were. They said that I had been a very special little baby. I was doing everything months before I should have. I was walking and talking and feeding myself with a shrimp fork, and then my mother bumped the high chair and I got arrested. It arrested me and that's why I'm the way I am. That's why I spill lemonade and drop the paper towels into the sink. But I wasn't born that way. No, I wasn't.

LEIF. I had a twin brother. He was stillborn.

(Long beat.)

ALTHEA. Oh well, my goodness.

(Long beat.)

LEIF. Mattie's right. There's no baby. That first home pregnancy test lied. She took a second test and it said no baby. Look, I finished a gondola.

ALTHEA. That's wonderful, dear. Would you like to stop now? Maybe you'd like to wait for your wife upstairs where you can be alone for a while.

LEIF. I have a better idea: why don't I just keep working on the puzzle?

ALTHEA. I just thought—

LEIF. *(Half serious, half facetious.)* In fact, I can think of nothing I'd rather do right now than teach this cheeky three-thousand-piecer a hard lesson. The absolute *nerve*, defying us this way!

ALTHEA. *(Swept up by **LEIF**'s more positive tone.)* Those Venetians are being *awfully* nervy, aren't they?

> *(Stops herself.)*

Wait. What about Connie?

LEIF. What *about* Connie? Last time I checked, her fingers were working just fine. It will be good therapy for the both of us. Otherwise, we're just gonna go home and spend the rest of the evening moping around, feeling sorry for ourselves.

ALTHEA. Well, you're both welcome to stay here for as long as you like.

LEIF. We'll call out for pizza. My treat.

ALTHEA. Of course, Mattie will have to keep the pizza far away from the table.

> *(**MATTIE** nods, smiles.)*

MATTIE. *(To **LEIF**.)* Did he look just like you?

LEIF. Who?

MATTIE. Your twin brother who was born real still.

LEIF. I don't know. My parents never told me. They never told me much about him at all. Didn't even give him a name. I used to think about him a lot. Wondered what it might have been like to have a twin brother. But to my mother and father, it was as if he'd never been born.

MATTIE. I sometimes think about having a twin sister. I know she'd be much, much smarter than me. I don't think my mother would have dropped *both* of us on our heads, do you?

LEIF. How could she be smarter than *you*, Mattie? You're a human RAM drive!

MATTIE. *(Privately, to* **ALTHEA.***)* Is that good?

ALTHEA. I think that's *very* good, sweetie.

LEIF. *(Turning to* **ALTHEA.***)* Connie had two miscarriages. Her first marriage. Maybe that's why she can't get pregnant now. Maybe it's for the best. If she *did* get pregnant, I know we'd be worrying the whole time that she'd lose this one just like the other two.

ALTHEA. Most miscarriages, dear – they happen for a reason. Should the baby have gone to term, there might have been terrible complications. This is nature's way of sparing the parents from certain heartache.

LEIF. So, we get the heartache on the front end instead. Ms. Witlin—

ALTHEA. *(Interrupting.)* Now, I told you to call me Althea.

LEIF. Do you see the bright side to *everything*?

ALTHEA. *(After some thought.)* No.

　　　(Beat.)

I don't, for example, think we're going to finish this jigsaw puzzle before my sister gets here.

LEIF. *(Trying to understand.)* This puzzle has become important to you.

ALTHEA. Well, in the universal scheme of things, it *shouldn't* be. But I simply can't help myself. I wander through these rooms, and for good or bad, I know that I *am* these rooms. I am this house. I am this silly, audacious puzzle. I am all the things that in very short order I won't get to be anymore.

MATTIE. *(Statement cum question.)* Your sister Ina – she doesn't like jigsaw puzzles.

ALTHEA. *(Nodding.)* My sister Ina doesn't like jigsaw puzzles, yes. Especially ones this big. She would not have the Grand Canal of Venice spread all over her dining room table.

MATTIE. Why are you going there? You don't have to go there. It isn't a good place for you to be.

ALTHEA. I have no choice, Mattie. I've explained this to you.

MATTIE. You can move in with *me.*

ALTHEA. *(Gentle laughter.)* Oh, wouldn't *we* be a pair!

MATTIE. Or you can stay here and I can move in with *you.*

ALTHEA. Honey, I will soon require care. I will not subject you to the terrible inconvenience of having to be my nursemaid.

MATTIE. *(On* **LEIF***'s surprised reaction.)* Althea is sick.

ALTHEA. *(Explaining, to* **LEIF.***)* I'm not checking out tomorrow, but Dr. Elam says I'm on a certain *trajectory.*

MATTIE. I can be your nurse. I like nurse uniforms. They're very crisp.

ALTHEA. *(To* **MATTIE.***)* Let's just put that thought out of our heads, dear. Besides, I need the money from the sale of this house. Now Ina and I – we've worked it all out. I sell the house and I use the money to pay her for my room and board. I do not intend to be a financial burden to my sister.

> *(There is a long silence, each of the three communing with his or her thoughts, while*

continuing to work on the puzzle. Suddenly, **LEIF** *looks up. He's had an epiphany. He throws his hands up into the air in a theatriccal "Now hear this!" gesture. He now has* **ALTHEA** *and* **MATTIE**'s *attention.)*

LEIF. Ladies. I think we can do it.

ALTHEA. Do what?

LEIF. Finish this "Mother-of-all-jigsaw puzzles."

ALTHEA. You *do?*

LEIF. But it will require working through the night. What time do you have to be out of here tomorrow?

ALTHEA. Ina said she'd be here after lunch. She has a special luncheon she has to attend. She was coming over right after that.

LEIF. Good. That's perfect.

ALTHEA. Don't you have to go to work tomorrow?

LEIF. I'll call in sick. I hardly ever call in sick.

ALTHEA. What about Connie?

LEIF. I'll talk to Connie when she gets here.

ALTHEA. *(Embracing the idea.)* It's the only one I never finished.

LEIF. The only one?

ALTHEA. *(Nodding.)* To be very honest, I was quite unhappy to have to leave here without having even opened the box.

LEIF. Well, not only have we opened the box, but we've got two gondolas put together and half the border finished!

(He checks his watch.)

And it's hardly past eight o'clock.

MATTIE. Eight o'clock! I have to feed Mr. Puss!

ALTHEA. Hurry back, dear.

MATTIE. *(Excitedly.)* I'll be right back.

> *(MATTIE crosses downstage while lights go out on ALTHEA and LEIF at the ping pong/puzzle table. A pin spot narrows on MATTIE, who now faces the audience. She holds an opened can of cat food in one hand and a spoon in the other.)*

(Continued, speaking to the audience.) I don't have any special way to work a jigsaw puzzle. I wish I did. I wish there was some kind of trick I could tell you about, like the tricks I learned at the group home for how to get spaghetti stains out of linoleum. That would be lemon juice and elbow grease.

> *(Beat, smiles.)*

Elbow grease isn't a real grease. It's what you say when you work hard. Well, that's what you do with a jigsaw puzzle, I guess: you give it a whole lot of elbow grease! Work, work, work, work, take a breath, go pee-pee, work, work, eat some pizza – sausage and mushrooms – work, work, work. Get sleepy, have some coffee, feed your cat so he doesn't get grumpy, work, work, go pee-pee again, work, work. And then it's over and you can take it apart and put it away and go get some sleep and watch Animal Planet and *Fashion Nine One One.* Is that a trick? I'm not sure. Althea has nimble fingers.

> *(She twiddles her fingers.)*

Have you noticed?

> *(Lights go down here and come up on the basement. CONNIE MORRELL stands near the door, flanked by LEIF and ALTHEA, who*

leave her standing there as they return to the
puzzle table.)

CONNIE. *(To* **LEIF,** *slightly confounded.)* So this is the –?

LEIF. I believe its official name is...

(Checking the box.)

... *Bells of the Campanile.*

ALTHEA. What a pretty name!

CONNIE. It's all one puzzle?

LEIF. *(Nodding.)* It's the mother-of-all-puzzles.

*(**MATTIE** now enters, breathless.)*

MATTIE. I came as fast as I could. Mr. Puss is eating canned salmon. He probably won't even miss me.

*(**MATTIE** studies **CONNIE**.)*

LEIF. Mattie, this is my wife Connie. Connie, this is Mattie.

CONNIE. Yes, from the phone.

*(**CONNIE** holds out a hand to shake.)*

MATTIE. My hands are sticky and I think there's cat food under my fingernails.

*(**CONNIE** retracts her hand. **MATTIE** goes to the puzzle. She turns and mimes shaking hands.)*

It's so nice to meet you.

LEIF. Mattie lives next door.

ALTHEA. *(To* **MATTIE**.) We just learned something, dear. The puzzle has a name: *Bells of the Campanile.* Isn't that a lovely name?

MATTIE. *(Examining the cover of the box.)* Where are the bells?

LEIF. I think they're in the tower.

MATTIE. *(Straining.)* I don't see them.

LEIF. I suppose we'll just have to imagine that's where they are.

CONNIE. Your house is really beautiful, Ms. Witlin.

ALTHEA. Thank you, dear.

MATTIE. I think I can hear them.

> *(She tick-tocks her head as if it were a swinging bell.)*

CONNIE. *(To LEIF.)* I thought you were still here because of the house. I didn't know you were here because of a jigsaw puzzle.

LEIF. Maybe I'm still here because I like this house *and* I like this puzzle.

CONNIE. Leif, I don't understand.

MATTIE. *(Closely examining the picture on the puzzlebox.)* Oh, oh, oh, oh! I think I see them now.

> *(**CONNIE** begins to cry.)*

Uh oh.

> *(**LEIF** goes to **CONNIE** and holds her.)*

LEIF. Oh, pumpkin!

> *(Comforting her.)*

Look. I *know.*

CONNIE. *(Through tears.)* How?

LEIF. Mattie told me.

CONNIE. Mattie?

LEIF. She overheard Beth. I'm so sorry, honey.

CONNIE. Those tests aren't supposed be wrong.

LEIF. *(Shaking his head.)* Of course they can be wrong. I read the disclaimer. It's rare, but you *can* occasionally get a false positive.

ALTHEA. *(To CONNIE.)* Did you do a third one, dear? Best two out of three?

CONNIE. Yes. At my Aunt Arlene's. The verdict's in.

> *(To LEIF.)*

I didn't know you liked jigsaw puzzles.

LEIF. Well, it's something we just never shared with each other.

CONNIE. It's a strange thing to like. I mean, it's very low tech.

LEIF. I have a low-tech side too, pumpkin.

> *(CONNIE moves toward the table. LEIF follows.)*

CONNIE. *(Scrutinizing their progress.)* You finished the gondolas.

LEIF. *(Proudly.)* That one's mine. The other one's Althea's.

CONNIE. There are too many people in that boat. It's liable to capsize.

> *(CONNIE picks up a piece and starts to scout its location.)*

This is very blue. Where's a spot that's very blue?

> *(ALTHEA picks up the box and studies the picture on the top.)*

ALTHEA. There's a glimmer of bright blue beneath that foot bridge.

CONNIE. Yes, I see it. Well, I'll put it down but there's nothing to connect it to. It's just going to float there by itself.

ALTHEA. *(Warmly.)* Then you'll simply have to locate its companions.

(**CONNIE** *turns to* **LEIF**.)

CONNIE. *(Matter-of-factly.)* You know we're going to be childless, don't you?

LEIF. We can adopt.

CONNIE. I wanted my own. A little girl with my hair and your eyes.

LEIF. What if she'd gotten *my* hair and *your* eyes?

CONNIE. There is nothing wrong with my eyes.

LEIF. *(Darkly playful.)* They're actually a little bloodshot at the moment. I prefer them, you know, a little less veiny.

ALTHEA. *(To* **LEIF**.*)* Shame on you! Connie's eyes are beautiful.

(Confidentially.)

Do you want me to get you some Visine, dear?

(**CONNIE** *shakes her head.*)

CONNIE. *(Suddenly becoming distracted.)* This piece is sticky.

LEIF. There was an accident.

(**MATTIE** *begins making th-th sounds with her flicking tongue.*)

ALTHEA. Mattie, dear, what are you doing?

MATTIE. The pigeons are taking off from the plaza. Cover your heads.

(She turns to **CONNIE**.*)*

Sorry about your loss.

*(***CONNIE*** *smiles sadly and turns to* **LEIF**.*)*

CONNIE. When are we going home?

LEIF. Probably about three o'clock tomorrow afternoon.

*(***CONNIE*** *gives him a quizzical look.)*

Unless we finish it sooner.

*(***CONNIE*** *continues to stare at* **LEIF**.*)*

CONNIE. Will we eat?

MATTIE. Pizza.

ALTHEA. And soon.

MATTIE. Good. I'm *starving*!

ALTHEA. And I'll make egg and cheese McMuffins tomorrow morning.

CONNIE. *(To* **LEIF**.*)* Will we sleep?

LEIF. Probably not.

ALTHEA. No rest for the weary! Look, look! I found his pole. I found the gondolier's missing pole.

CONNIE. *(To* **LEIF**.*)* And we're doing this because...?

LEIF. Because it's Venice. Because we've never been to Venice before. Because I love you...

(He kisses her.)

...and I very much need you right by my side tonight. All night long. And I'm going to take myself a little guess...

(He pinches **CONNIE***'s nose with affection.)*

...that just maybe you need me too.

> (**CONNIE** *backs away from the table. She mulls this over, then makes a decision; she rolls up her sleeves, pulls her hair back out of her face and returns in earnest to the puzzle.*)

CONNIE. I like mushroom. With red pepper.

> (*To* **LEIF.**)

Step back a little, honey. You're in my light.

> (*Lights fade out.*)

End of Act One

ACT TWO

(Much later that evening. The puzzle-working quartet is still hard at work. The bar stools now surround the table, with the foursome popping up and down, standing, then sitting, then getting up again and moving about the table – each member of the ensemble in constant motion. Open pizza boxes now litter the bar counter, along with a half-finished liters of soda, and plastic cups. **LEIF** *goes to the bar, snatches a couple of bites from one of the remaining pizza slices, wipes his fingers up and down the wet paper towel roll, then returns to the puzzle. All the while we hear the sound of the radio, which has been switched on.)*

MAN'S VOICE. Betty from Portland, Maine: you're on the air.

BETTY'S VOICE. Charlie, I don't know why in the world you let this man back on your show.

CHARLIE'S VOICE. I thought my listeners deserved *some* kind of explanation. Which, incidentally, he has yet to give me. Mr. Armbruster, here we are now firmly ensconced in the new millennium and the earth hasn't ended as you predicted. What do you have to say for yourself?

ARMBRUSTER'S VOICE. I didn't say it was going to happen right on New Year's Day.

BETTY'S VOICE. Yes, you did! I heard that show! I heard every word of it. Armageddon and the Rapture and cherubim and seraphim. Well, I'm still here. I'm not in Heaven. Nothing has changed. I'm still married to the laziest bum in America, and I still can't even look at Mexican food without getting the runs.

(**ALTHEA** *moves to the radio.*)

CHARLIE'S VOICE. Betty from Portland makes a good point, Mr. Armbruster.

(**ALTHEA** *turns the radio dial.*)

ALTHEA. I cannot listen to another minute of this!

(**ALTHEA** *switches the radio to music: an "easy listening" format. She lowers the volume.**)

CONNIE. This has got to be a new low for your station, Leif. You really ought to ask Delaney why he insists on running these freakazoid talk shows in the middle of the night.

LEIF. *A*: they're syndicated. They're cheap. And *B*: a lot of people just happen to like this kind of programming.

ALTHEA. Connie makes a good point, Leif. Charlie's guests are even more freakazoid tonight than usual.

(**MATTIE** *is falling asleep on her bar stool.*)

Mattie, dear, you're listing.

(**MATTIE** *straightens up. She shakes herself awake.*)

And you've got pizza sauce all over your chin.

---

* A license to produce THE PUZZLE WITH THE PIAZZA does not include a performance license for any third-party or copyrighted music. Licensees should create an original composition or use music in the public domain. For further information, please see Music Use Note on page 3.

> *(She grabs a stray paper towel and wipes* **MATTIE**'s *chin.* **CONNIE** *starts chuckling to herself.)*

LEIF. *(To* **CONNIE**.*) What?*

CONNIE. Mattie. She's the "Leaning Tower of *Pizza*."

> *(***MATTIE** *likes this. She starts giggling.)*

ALTHEA. *(To* **MATTIE**.*)* Would you like to go upstairs and lie down for a while?

MATTIE. I'm okay. I'm just not used to staying up this late.

ALTHEA. When is it you usually get to bed, dear?

MATTIE. About nine-thirty.

ALTHEA. *(Consulting her watch.)* It's well past midnight. Are you going to be all right?

MATTIE. *(Nodding.)* I have ways of staying awake.

> *(She sings softly to herself.)*

"ABA DABA DABA DABA DABA DABA DAB", said the chimpy to the monk.

> *(She makes a monkey mouth by placing her tongue behind her upper lip.* **CONNIE** *makes the same mouth and the two fall to giggles.)*

LEIF. *(Getting a fun idea.)* Hey, hey, hey, hey! Who am *I*?

> *(He snatches up one of the pizza boxes, tucks it under his arm, squats down on his haunches, and orients his hands in front of him in the manner of a baseball catcher.)*

CONNIE. *(Indulgent.)* I don't know. *(She tosses it over to* **ALTHEA** *and* **MATTIE**. *They both shrug.)*

LEIF. This one was *soooo* easy. I'm Mike Piazza! I'm *Mike Piazza with a pizza!*

ALTHEA. *(Sweetly.)* I don't know who that is.

LEIF. Mets catcher.

> *(Getting up.)*

Phenomenal catcher for the Mets. I'd have him at *my* dinner party in a New York minute. Hey! *New York* minute!

(Continued, to **CONNIE.***)* Did you get that, pumpkin?

CONNIE. I got it. We all got it.

> *(She pats her husband patronizingly on the arm.)*

ALTHEA. *(To* **CONNIE.***)* Before we checked in with "Armageddon Armbruster," you were going to tell me how you and Leif met.

CONNIE. *(Recalling it makes her smile.)* It was Petey's Putt Putt at Summer and Spruce.

LEIF. I was there with my friends, and Connie was there with *her* friends. Connie's group was right behind *my* group – nipping at our heels.

> *(During the following,* **MATTIE** *continues to fight off sleep.)*

CONNIE. Leif and his bunch were acting like eight-year-olds.

LEIF. *(An explanation.)* It was only Jarrell. Jarrell was trying to impress Sheila. He was playing all the holes with his eyes taped shut.

CONNIE. *(An aside to* **ALTHEA.***)* Sheila wasn't impressed.

LEIF. This gave Connie and me the chance to meet. To get to know each other.

CONNIE. And one thing led to another.

LEIF. Bottom line is she asked *me* out.

ALTHEA. Sadie Hawkins in the putt-putt park!

CONNIE. He was so shy, Althea. I knew that if I wasn't the one to make the move, we might never see each other again.

> (**MATTIE***'s head has dropped to the table. She now seems to be asleep.* **ALTHEA** *notices.*)

ALTHEA. Oh dear. What should we do?

LEIF. Let her have her little nap. Maybe it'll revive her.

ALTHEA. The last time I remember staying up all night – I mean, on *purpose* – I won't count all the nights I would have liked nothing better than to drift peacefully off – well, the last time was when my husband – rather, my *ex*-husband – was in I.C.U. The night before he died. I was on the phone, trying to find Collin. My stomach was tied in knots.

LEIF. *(Tenderly, to* **ALTHEA.***)* How about we replace *that* one with *this* one?

ALTHEA. What a nice idea! This *has* been such a lovely evening.

LEIF. And it's hardly half over.

CONNIE. *(Unhappy, indicating* **MATTIE.***)* She's on my basilica. She's got her head resting right on the domes of my basilica.

ALTHEA. *(To* **CONNIE.***)* Come help me with the canal. This water looks so dirty. I'm surprised Katharine Hepburn didn't get some sort of amoebic infection.

CONNIE. I'm ready for ice cream. Leif, I'm going to the Handy Mandy and get us all some ice cream. What flavor would everybody like?

ALTHEA. Just don't get that ice milk. It tastes like flavored water.

CONNIE. *(Nodding.)* Or frozen yogurt. I hate the way frozen yogurt gets all uppity like, *I'm just as cold-comfort tasty as ice cream is!* Well, guess what? You're *not*!

LEIF. Connie, I don't want you going by yourself.

> *(Glancing at his watch.)*

It's almost one o'clock.

ALTHEA. *(To* **LEIF.***)* She'll be fine, dear. The Handy Mandy's just around the corner, and Officer Perry's almost always sitting right out front in his patrol car. One night when I couldn't sleep, he invited me to sit with him. We listened to the police radio and ate Funyuns.

> *(Extracting herself from the pleasant memory.)*

Anyway, I like vanilla.

CONNIE. I know Leif likes chocolate. And I like strawberry. What does Mattie like?

ALTHEA. Mattie is lactose-intolerant, dear.

CONNIE. She just ate half a pizza.

ALTHEA. You know, I didn't even think about that.

LEIF. She seemed to be pretty diligent about picking off that cheese. Maybe she'll be all right.

ALTHEA. When I was a girl, we had another name for that Neapolitan ice cream.

LEIF. *(Nodding; he knows it.)* Van-choc-straw.

> *(***ALTHEA** *registers surprise.)*

Van for vanilla. Choc for chocolate. And straw...

ALTHEA. For strawberry. Oh Lord, it's like you were *there*!

> *(***MATTIE** *raises her head.)*

MATTIE. *(Groggily.)* Van-choc-straw!

(She smiles pleasantly, then returns to hibernation.)

ALTHEA. *(To* **LEIF** *and* **CONNIE.***)* You know, sometimes I look at the two of you and it's like I've always known you. It's almost as if you were seated right next to Ina and me on my granddaddy's splintery old porch, all four of us waiting for Ol' Whipple-toes to dish up the VCS. He always used this special soda fountain ice cream scoop he stole from Woolworth's.

CONNIE. Who was "Ol' Whipple-toes"?

ALTHEA. My bachelor uncle. Whip. He spoiled Ina and me terribly. He was so good to us. He stole things, though.

LEIF. Like ice-cream scoops.

ALTHEA. *(Nodding.)* And Lincoln Continentals. *One* Lincoln Continental. Right off the lot. He went straight to prison. Did not pass go. Did not collect even a goodbye from Ina and me. And that's where he died. He slipped in the shower and irreparably damaged his brain stem. Oh Lord, now *I'm* the one giving too much information.

CONNIE. There's been so much tragedy in your life.

ALTHEA. Oh honey, doesn't every life have its moments of sadness and misfortune? The bad days make the good days seem even better, don't you think? Anyway: been very good at negotiating my way around all the obstacles that life has put in front of me. No, that isn't the hard part.

LEIF. What's the hard part?

CONNIE. *(Chastising.)* She was getting to the hard part. Don't interrupt her.

LEIF. *(With an exaggerated mea-culpa gesture of the hands.) Sorry.*

CONNIE. *(Repenting.)* No, *I'm* sorry.

> *(She kisses* **LEIF** *on the cheek.)*

I've got the one-o'clock grumps. What's the hard part, Althea?

ALTHEA. It's the gaps, dear. All those terrible gaps.

CONNIE. Gaps?

ALTHEA. Those big empty spaces that glare at you when you step back and take stock. Uncle Whip wasn't a gap. He was a positive – yes, criminal – but mostly positive force in my life. The gaps are the things left undone, left unsaid, opportunities missed, chances that never came, or that got all botched up. Regrets that look just like my late husband. I should never have married him. I should never have run over my son in the driveway. It just added to that wedge between us. But you can't spend the rest of your days playing the "should've/could've" game. Because it's a game you can never win. You have to stop playing that game and try to live as best you can in the moments you have left, in spite of all the holes that riddle your life like Swiss cheese. Because all of our lives are big chunks of Swiss cheese, aren't they?

> *(***CONNIE*** nods.)*

CONNIE. I'm – it's very hard trying not to think about the baby.

ALTHEA. Yes, I know.

CONNIE. Because I know now – in my heart – that it's just never going to happen.

> *(She turns to* **LEIF.***)*

We don't get to be whole, Leif. Not the way we always wanted.

(**LEIF** *goes to* **CONNIE.**)

LEIF. We don't have to give up, pumpkin.

> (**CONNIE** *shakes her head. She takes a deep breath.*)

CONNIE. It's time we stopped trying. It's time we turned the page, Leif. I'm going to get ice cream. I feel like eating lots of van-choc-straw. Mostly straw, but let me have a taste of your van and your choc, and I'll be a happy member of the – what was that name we gave ourselves?

ALTHEA. "Puzzle Platoon."

CONNIE. (*To* **ALTHEA.**) Permission to procure some VCS, Sergeant?

ALTHEA. Permission granted, Private.

> (*They exchange salutes.* **CONNIE** *exits.*)

LEIF. (*Calling after her.*) I still vote for "Gondolier Brigade."

> (*Lights go down. A narrow pin spot comes up on* **CONNIE** *elsewhere on stage. She holds a plastic bag which, by the shape of it, appears to contain a box-shaped object that could very well be a carton of ice cream. She addresses the audience.*)

CONNIE. I've never worked a jigsaw puzzle before. You have to believe this, although it seems too strange, doesn't it? I missed the boat on that one. I've never seen *Casablanca* either. Or visited the Grand Canyon *or* Disney World. I don't like to fly, and when I was little, I would get deathly carsick. I mean, so carsick that I couldn't go ten miles without revisiting everything I'd eaten since I got up that morning. Okay, T.M.I., right? Anyway, that makes me the last person to be giving you advice on the best way to put together a ridiculously large jigsaw puzzle. Although I *have* been at this one long enough to offer a *couple* of pointers. First, it helps if you don't concentrate *too* closely on the task at hand. The brain's a funny organ; it doesn't always need every synapse of attention to its job. Sometimes it works best when switched to automatic pilot. The second thing I've noticed about working puzzles is that it helps to have people working it with you. It helps a lot. You draw from one another. It's hard to describe.

> *(Beat.)*

It's funny.

> *(Beat.)*

I don't want this night to end.

> *(Lights fade out. In the darkness we hear a loud female yelp. When the lights come back up in the basement, we see the aftermath of a little accident.* **MATTIE***'s stool is overturned. The ping pong table has buckled slightly in the middle. There is a scattering of puzzle pieces on the floor, which have spilled through the gap in the middle of the table.* **ALTHEA,** **LEIF,** *and* **MATTIE** *stand, surveying the damage.* **CONNIE** *is at the door, bag in hand.)*

CONNIE. What happened?

MATTIE. *(Distraught.)* I was too heavy. I was sleeping and I was too heavy and the weight of me – of my big head – it was too much for the table – and then the table – and then the table –

ALTHEA. *(Calmly.)* It's really not that bad, dear.

> **(LEIF** *starts to adjust the legs of the table so that the top sits flat again.)*

LEIF. We'll get everything right back to where it was in a New York minute!

> (**CONNIE** *sets the bag of ice cream on the bar counter and goes to assist* **MATTIE** *in picking up the spilled puzzle pieces.*)

MATTIE. I – I – I think I should go home now.

CONNIE. It's okay, Mattie. We've all got it covered.

> (**MATTIE** *sits down on the floor. She clutches puzzle pieces in her fists.*)

MATTIE. I'll just go and do something else bad. You don't need me helping you anymore.

ALTHEA. Nonsense!

> (**ALTHEA** *holds out her palms.* **MATTIE** *deposits the puzzle pieces she's collected into* **ALTHEA**'s *hands.*)

You are – in spite of your big, heavy ol' head – *still* the best puzzle worker in this room.

> (**MATTIE** *shakes her head slowly and sadly. She gets up. She starts for the door.* **LEIF** *and* **CONNIE** *and* **ALTHEA** *trade looks of concern.*)

LEIF. *(Calling to* **MATTIE**.*)* Fourteen ninety-two.

> (**MATTIE** *stops.*)

MATTIE. *(Obligingly.)* Thirty-eight point six two six four.

LEIF. Sixteen hundred and sixty-six.

MATTIE. Forty point eight one six five. You have to stop doing this. I have to go.

LEIF. You can't go. There are still fifty more square roots I need to learn.

MATTIE. You can use your calculator.

LEIF. I'd rather use *you*. You're an invaluable resource, Mattie. You are very much needed here tonight.

(**MATTIE** *thinks this over.*)

MATTIE. The square root of sixteen-sixty-six isn't forty point eight one six five. It's forty point eight one six *six*. I got it wrong because I'm a little sleepy.

(*Beat.*)

I have to go to the bathroom.

ALTHEA. I'll go with you, dear.

LEIF. Keep a close watch on that one, Althea. She's a definite flight risk.

(**MATTIE** *and* **ALTHEA** *exit.* **LEIF** *and* **CONNIE** *finish picking up the rest of the errant pieces and return them to the table. A silence passes as they flip the restored pieces one-by-one face-up upon the table.*)

You sure you want us to stop trying to –? [have a baby]

(**CONNIE** *nods.*)

Can we at least *talk* about adoption?

CONNIE. (*Stroking* **LEIF**'s *cheek affectionately.*) We can talk about it.

LEIF. But not now?

CONNIE. Not now. It's late. I'm very tired.

LEIF. Pumpkin, you want me to take you home?

CONNIE. If I wanted to go home, I could drive myself home. Do *you* want to go home?

LEIF. Well, *no*.

CONNIE. Then we stay and see this out.

(Pointing.)

You flipped that one the wrong way.

(He nods and re-flips the piece.)

(Continued, after a beat.) What does it mean?

LEIF. What does *what* mean?

CONNIE. This puzzle. I know why *we're* doing it. We're doing it for Althea. Why is *she* doing it?

LEIF. Because it's the only puzzle she hasn't –

CONNIE. *(Interrupting.)* No. I want the real reason.

LEIF. I don't know, pumpkin. Maybe it really *is* one of the last things she feels like she'll have any control over.

CONNIE. *(Expanding on this.)* A loss of agency, of a sense of self-empowerment. Fighting to hold on to whatever shreds of—

LEIF. I think you're overthinking this.

CONNIE. I do that, don't I? Overthink things.

(Suddenly arch.)

Whereas Leif Morrell *never* overthinks things.

LEIF. We should both stop it. It just makes us crazy.

CONNIE. Yes, I know.

(Her voice softening.)

I'd like to just stop thinking, period. Leif, for once I'd just like to *be*.

LEIF. So *be*. Be my wife, be my honey, be my sunny, eternal, everlasting soulmate. How about we learn how to stop and smell the roses, but without trying to pull off all the petals?

(He gives her a kiss.)

CONNIE. That's what we do?

LEIF. *(Nodding.)* We're standing around with a bunch of thorny stems, you and me.

CONNIE. Sometimes all I want in the world is just to be with you. Just the two of us. But there are times, Leif, when I need *other* people in my life. And I look around, and nobody's there.

LEIF. You have your sister Beth. Your Aunt Arlene.

CONNIE. And that's *it*, really. My circle is small, Leif – *our* circle. I don't know how it got to be that way. We're decent people. Where *is* everybody?

LEIF. Maybe we closed ourselves off a little too much. All the funerals last year. It was like some kind of never-ending Greek tragedy.

CONNIE. I hear the phone ring in the middle of the night, my whole body goes limp. I want life again, Leif. I'm tired of death. This baby – this baby was going to be life.

LEIF. I know.

> *(**LEIF** holds **CONNIE** close for a moment. She pulls slightly away. Something makes her smile.)*

What is it?

CONNIE. Althea.

> *(He considers her curiously.)*

I like her.

LEIF. I do too. *And* Mattie.

CONNIE. Yes. It's such a strange thing.

LEIF. What?

CONNIE. To warm so easily to two people you just met. After such a long period of warming to no one.

LEIF. Kindred strangers.

CONNIE. I like that.

(*She kisses him.*)

LEIF. You taste like pizza.

CONNIE. (*Grinning, pointing to the bag of ice cream on the bar counter.*) And the ice cream cometh!

(*They laugh. Lights fade here and come up elsewhere on* **INA GLUCK.** *She is slightly younger than her sister* **ALTHEA,** *and wears a night robe.*)

INA. (*Speaking to the audience.*) I worked the damned things the summer I was ten. The summer Althea and I spent at sleep-away camp. It rained almost the whole time we were there. A veritable monsoon. And there was nothing to do but read Nancy Drew and piece together those ancient jigsaw puzzles that smelled of must and baked beans. I grew to hate the blasted things. So, for me to stand here in the middle of the night and share perky tips on how to conquer the jigsaw in record time – well, honey, you get absolutely no buy-in from *me*! What I *will* tell you about the jigsaw puzzle is that it's the most inane, useless, mind-numbing pastime devised by man. It rivals solitaire and painting by numbers. Filling the void of the empty life. My life, as it so happens, is sufficiently full. So, I will leave the puzzles for those less blessed. Like my sister Althea. She has dozens of them. She's worked every one of them, I believe. When her husband died and after that terrible incident where she ran over my nephew with her car, she'd cocoon herself off in that dark, dank basement of hers and flick and snap those pieces together like some psychiatric patient, and I would try my best not to worry. Fortunately, she is now beyond the puzzle stage in her life's journey and I am happy for her. She is moving in with me, which will be additionally beneficial to her. This is a good thing.

(*Beat. She grins mischievously.*)

But if I *were* to offer advice on putting together the dreaded jigsaw puzzle, I would say this: you must force all the damned pieces together whether they were cut to fit or not. Take a hammer to the thing if necessary – finish it off in less than an hour. The result will be no beautiful picture, for certain, but the dirty deed *will* be done. Finished. Finis. Because the important thing *isn't* the picture, *isn't* the finished product. The important thing is just to be damned rid of it. Granted, this is an unorthodox approach, but certainly one which frees me – and you too, should you heed my advice – to devote time and attention to more important endeavors. Such as battening down one's hatches for the arrival of one's dear older sister. I exiled all peace and sanity the day I agreed to let her come live with me. Do I rue the decision?

(*She thinks about this.*)

"Rue" is such a *harsh* word.

(*Lights fade out and come back up in the basement.* **LEIF**, **MATTIE** *and* **CONNIE** *are working the puzzle.* **ALTHEA** *fiddles with the radio knob, bouncing among stations before settling on one that plays classical music.** *It's a piece with a certain drive to it. A nearly empty box of Neapolitan ice cream sits on the bar, surrounded by dirty bowls and spoons.*)

**A license to produce THE PUZZLE WITH THE PIAZZA does not include a performance license for any third-party or copyrighted music. Licensees should create an original composition or use music in the public domain. For further information, please see Music Use Note on page 3.

CONNIE. That's good. Right there.

LEIF. I'd prefer the *William Tell Overture* or *Flight of the Bumblebee* but this is almost as good.

> (**ALTHEA** *returns to the table.*)

ALTHEA. We shouldn't push ourselves too hard or we're liable to tire out. How are *you* holding up, Mattie?

MATTIE. I'm fine. We need a window. I'll bet the sun is coming up and we can't even see it.

LEIF. Toiling away in our subterranean darkness.

> (*Indicating the puzzle.*)

Looks great, Mattie!

> (*To the others.*)

Mattie finished the piazza. Mattie, there's a little pizza on your piazza.

CONNIE. (*To* **LEIF**.) The piazza jokes are getting stale, sweetie.

MATTIE. I can't find that one piece.

> (*She points.*)

Right there.

LEIF. It'll turn up.

CONNIE. I'm a little nauseous.

ALTHEA. You ate too much ice cream.

CONNIE. Maybe it's phantom morning sickness.

> (*Everyone turns and stares at* **CONNIE**.)

I was making a joke. I can make that joke because I'm taking ownership of my pain.

LEIF. *(To* **ALTHEA** *and* **MATTIE**.*)* Connie reads books. Connie, honey, you need to stop reading books.

> *(Squeezing the back of his neck.)*

I have an idea. Why don't you massage the back of my neck?

> (**CONNIE** *pulls herself away from the puzzle to massage* **LEIF**'s *neck.*)

MATTIE. *(Monkey see, monkey do.)* Massage my neck, Althea.

> (**ALTHEA** *takes herself from the puzzle to massage* **MATTIE**'s *neck.*)

ALTHEA. *(To* **LEIF**.*)* Honey, could you...?

> (**LEIF** *begins, obligingly, to massage* **ALTHEA**'s *neck.* **MATTIE** *edges toward* **CONNIE** *and begins to massage her neck so that a neck-massaging circle has been formed.*)

LEIF. I'll bet this looks a little kinky.

ALTHEA. *(Tickled.)* If Ina walked in right now, I cannot imagine what she would think.

> *(The circle begins to move so that the foursome are now in locomotion. They all start laughing, and chugging faster.)*

MATTIE. *(A train whistle.)* Whoo! Whoo!

CONNIE. I'm going to throw up! I'm about to throw up!

> (**CONNIE** *wrenches herself away and goes to the folding chair to sit down.*)

ALTHEA. *(The nurse.)* Put your head between your legs, dear.

(**CONNIE** *does as instructed. All but* **CONNIE** *return to the puzzle.*)

(Continued, to **CONNIE**.*)* Better?

CONNIE. *(Raising her head.)* If your preference is for me to throw up on my shoes.

LEIF. Connie has a straw stomach.

CONNIE. Leif has a misplaced nipple.

ALTHEA. A what?

CONNIE. A misplaced nipple.

LEIF. *(Closing his eyes in mortification, to* **CONNIE**.*)* Did you have to go and –? [tell them that]

ALTHEA. I don't know what that means.

MATTIE. *(To* **LEIF**.*)* You lost your nipple? Which one?

CONNIE. It's the one on the right. It's slightly up and to the left of where it ought to be—symmetrically speaking.

ALTHEA. *(To* **LEIF**.*)* Is it a congenital defect, dear?

LEIF. I guess. Supposedly, my twin brother had the same thing on the opposite side.

MATTIE. I'd like to see it.

ALTHEA. *(Admonishing.)* Mattie!

LEIF. Maybe some other time.

CONNIE. *(Returning to the puzzle, to* **LEIF**.*)* What will it hurt to show them?

(*To* **ALTHEA** *and* **MATTIE**.*)*

It takes some getting used to, but you won't regret the experience.

LEIF. Connie, *please.*

CONNIE. You're always telling me how little it matters to you. That it's the way God made you.

LEIF. *(Acquiescing.)* Well, you can't have any more fun with me than the boys in school did. All right. I can't believe I'm doing this.

> (**LEIF**, *with his back to audience, lifts his shirt and presents his chest to the three women.* **ALTHEA** *and* **MATTIE** *inspect it with almost morbid interest.)*

ALTHEA. Oh, Lord, honey, it really *isn't* where it ought to be, is it?

LEIF. I'm damaged goods, right?

ALTHEA. *(Dismissing this.)* We all have little body quirks. The baby toe on my left foot has no nail.

> (**LEIF** *lowers his shirt.)*

MATTIE. Did it *ever* have a nail?

> *(They all return to the puzzle.)*

ALTHEA. Not that I'm aware.

CONNIE. *(Mordantly.)* I have a deficiency of the womb.

LEIF. *(Chastising.)* Stop.

ALTHEA. Pink.

CONNIE. What?

ALTHEA. A while ago you asked me my favorite color and I said I'd never thought about it. And now I *have* thought about it and I will say pink. But a deep, dark, dramatic shade of pink.

CONNIE. Like a Pepto-Bismol pink?

MATTIE. No, no. Althea means like a beautiful pink sunset.

ALTHEA. Or sun*rise*. Mattie's right: we could be missing a gorgeous sunrise this morning.

LEIF. The sun will rise on another day. Nobody leaves this table.

CONNIE. Golda Meir and Madeleine Albright.

ALTHEA. Would you seat them next to each other?

CONNIE. Of course.

MATTIE. Gilligan and Sue Anne Nivens and Ms. Jeanine Pokorski.

ALTHEA. *(To* **MATTIE.***)* Who is Mrs. Jeanine Pokorski, dear?

MATTIE. She's the lady who came to the group home and taught us how to color-coordinate our wardrobes.

CONNIE. *(To* **MATTIE.***)* And why would she be a good guest for your dinner party?

MATTIE. I liked the way she smiled. She had a nice smile. She can sit at the head of my table and smile and make everybody feel welcome.

ALTHEA. Do you see her anymore, dear?

MATTIE. No. She died. You said I could have dead people.

ALTHEA. You can have whoever you want, sweetie.

MATTIE. Then I also want Cinderella and Snow White. Connie gets Goldilocks.

CONNIE. *(Correcting her.)* Not *Goldilocks*. Golda *Meir*.

LEIF. Blue. Forget khaki. I was kidding with khaki.

CONNIE. Khaki isn't even a color. You were trying to be clever.

LEIF. It certainly *is* a color.

CONNIE. It's a color-*like* entity.

LEIF. It's a state of mind.

ALTHEA. *Adam's Rib. Philadelphia Story.*

LEIF. I think you named *Philadelphia Story* already.

MATTIE. Was Katharine Hepburn in *Westward the Women*? I like that one. There was this wagon train and it was almost all women. I'll bet one of them was Katharine Hepburn.

CONNIE. *The Madwoman of... something.*

MATTIE. Of Main Street. *The Madwoman of Main Street.*

ALTHEA. *(With a grin, playing along.)* Who else was in that picture, Mattie?

MATTIE. Sophia Loren and Valerie Bertinelli.

ALTHEA. And what was it about, dear?

MATTIE. A woman who pulls her hair out and then goes looking for the beauty parlor.

ALTHEA. And why does she pull her hair out?

LEIF. *(Preoccupied.)* Because she's *mad*! Look! Finished this whole section.

MATTIE. Oh, that's good. Pull it over here. I bet it'll connect.

(They work to bring two sections together.)

ALTHEA. *(To* **MATTIE.**) You don't know why she pulls all of her hair out?

MATTIE. I do.

ALTHEA. *(Playfully.)* You're just going to keep it all to yourself? Maybe we'd like to see the movie.

MATTIE. I don't even think it's a real movie. I think it's a dream movie.

ALTHEA. Do you dream movies too? I thought I was the only one.

MATTIE. I dream movies that most people wouldn't want to see. Sometimes *I* don't even want to see them.

ALTHEA. And this was one of those movies?

(**MATTIE** *nods.*)

Am *I* in this movie, dear?

(**MATTIE** *nods again.*)

Now see, how did I know that?

MATTIE. Katharine Hepburn plays you in all of my head movies.

ALTHEA. Well, I appreciate the casting choice, dear. It shows you have good taste.

LEIF. Except for, you know, that invitation for Gilligan to come to her dinner party.

ALTHEA. So why is this *me* person in your dream movie – why is she so driven to pull her hair out? Can you tell me?

MATTIE. Because nobody likes it – her hair. They talk about it behind her back and sometimes they point at her –

ALTHEA. *(Clarifying.)* At *me.*

MATTIE. Yes. And so she pulls it out and then she goes to the beauty parlor and I – I put on my smock, and I make it all beautiful again.

CONNIE. *(Trying to understand.)* You give her a wig.

ALTHEA. *(Hit hard by this, a little numbed.)* Surely there must be little tufts left atop.

MATTIE. Little tufts, yes. And I take the tufts and I weave them with the beautiful wig hair – the soft natural hair that I have selected just for you and it all blends so wonderfully and you are quite pleased.

ALTHEA. *(Smiling.)* I'm pleased.

(**MATTIE** *nods.*)

But Mattie, that sounds like a *happy* ending.

(**MATTIE** *shakes her head.*)

MATTIE. You walk out of the beauty parlor and get run over by a bus.

>   (**ALTHEA** *doesn't respond. She goes and sits down.*)

>   (*Continued, to* **ALTHEA**.*)* I'm sorry. I was just telling you how it ended.

CONNIE. *(To* **MATTIE**.*)* That's an *awful* way to end your movie!

MATTIE. I – I probably shouldn't have –

ALTHEA. *(Softly.)* What kind of a –

MATTIE. It was a school bus.

LEIF. I think somebody ought to change the subject, like, *fast.*

CONNIE. *(Privately, to* **LEIF**.*)* But please: no more square root challenges, okay?

>   (**ALTHEA** *gets up.*)

ALTHEA. *(Still numb.)* I believe I'll go upstairs and lie down for a bit.

CONNIE. *(To* **ALTHEA**.*)* Are you sure you're okay?

ALTHEA. I'm getting a no-sleep headache, that's all. It will pass.

MATTIE. Do you want me to –

ALTHEA. *(Cutting her off; with forced cheer.)* Dear, you just keep working the puzzle. You're very good. And we've made excellent progress.

>   (**ALTHEA** *exits. The others stand motionless for a moment, pinned under the dark weight that has descended on the room.* **MATTIE**

begins to cry: a soft, delicate whimper, which she tries to suppress with the palm of her hand.)

CONNIE. *(To* **MATTIE,** *trying to comfort.)* You didn't understand –

MATTIE. I should never open my mouth.

(Beat.)

Except to eat.

(Beat.)

I can breathe out of my nose.

CONNIE. *(To* **LEIF.***)* Should I go up there?

LEIF. Why don't you wait? Maybe she just needs a little time to herself. We've been pretty much on top of each other all night.

MATTIE. Althea thinks that nobody needs her. *I* need her. I need her every day.

(To **CONNIE.***)*

When you go up and see her, will you tell her that? She thinks I can do all these things myself. I *can't*! I mess it all up.

LEIF. *(To* **MATTIE.***)* She's been very helpful to you, hasn't she?

MATTIE. I don't know what I'll do without her. I just don't know what I'll do.

(They return to working the puzzle in silence. Lights slowly fade to black. In the darkness

we hear music coming from the radio. It
*is a lively, catchy tune, and as lights come
back up, we see* **CONNIE**, **LEIF** *and* **MATTIE**
*mindlessly swaying and tapping their feet. A
moment later we hear, almost imperceptibly
under the music, the removed sound of*
ALTHEA's *front doorbell.* **MATTIE** *goes and
turns off the music.)*

MATTIE. Did you hear that?

CONNIE. Hear what?

LEIF. *(Nodding.)* Doorbell.

MATTIE. Someone is here.

LEIF. *(Shrugging it off.)* Somebody else for Althea to say
goodbye to.

MATTIE. *(Shaking her head.)* She came early.

CONNIE. Who came early?

MATTIE. *Her*!

LEIF. *(Understanding, explaining to* **CONNIE**.*)* The sister:
Ina.

MATTIE. Althea *thought* she might come early. She does
things early. She always gets the worm.

LEIF. *(A protest.)* But Althea hasn't had lunch. The sister is
supposed to let Althea have her lunch first.

CONNIE. *(Checking the time.)* It's eleven. Maybe that
important lunch of Ina's turned into a breakfast.

       (Beat.)

Somebody go upstairs and find out.

(*Nobody moves.*)

The suspense is going to kill me.

LEIF. We'll find out soon enough. Pick up the pace. Connie, you've spent forever on the sky. Let Mattie have the sky. You take the water.

CONNIE. I was doing the water most of the night. I like the pale blue of the sky.

LEIF. (*An order.*) Mattie, take the sky.

CONNIE. (*To* **LEIF.**) Who died and left you in charge?

LEIF. If we don't get organized here, the ship is sunk.

CONNIE. Aye aye, Captain Nipple.

(*A long silence.*)

It was probably just the man who cleans her eaves. She's telling *him* goodbye.

MATTIE. Maybe.

(*Straining.*)

I hear voices.

LEIF. (*As well.*) I hear Althea's.

CONNIE. And a man, right?

(**MATTIE,** *listening, shakes her head.*)

MATTIE. (*To* **CONNIE.**) Can I help you with the sky? There are supposed to be pigeons there, but I haven't found them yet.

CONNIE. (*Capitulating, with a dusting of sarcasm.*) Yes, by all means, let's put those pigeons in the sky.

(*To* **LEIF,** *with nervous glances at the door.*)

Look at me. My hand's shaking. I'm – I'm twelve years old again, and there's Aunt Edith upstairs with the gravelly voice and the goiter.

(**LEIF** *goes to* **CONNIE** *and puts his arm around her.*)

LEIF. *(Delicately.)* Your Aunt Edith's dead, pumpkin. She can never hurt you again.

CONNIE. She never hurt me. She just creeped me out. God, I need sleep.

MATTIE. Look! You've got a pigeon in your hand! Its wings are fluttering.

(*As* **CONNIE** *holds up the puzzle piece to examine it closer,* **ALTHEA** *enters. She is accompanied by* **INA GLUCK.**)

INA. *(To the three puzzle workers.)* Good morning.

(*Ad libbed "hello" and "good morning" from the trio.*)

ALTHEA. *(To* **INA.**) I give you: "the Puzzle Platoon." All present and accounted for, though not quite as bright-eyed and bushy-tailed as we'd like.

(*She stifles a yawn. To the others, indicating* **INA.**)

She didn't believe me.

INA. *(To* **ALTHEA.**) All *night*?

LEIF. Since early yesterday evening.

ALTHEA. *(Admiring the puzzle.)* It's really coming along.

(*To* **CONNIE.**)

Oh, look. You're moving back to the water. That's fine! It's your forte, dear.

INA. Are you going to introduce me to these people, Althea?

ALTHEA. I'm sorry. People, this is my sister, Ina. Ina, this is Mattie, but you've met her before.

INA. I don't recall.

MATTIE. I was out in the yard and we talked about roses and I – I – I wasn't looking where I was pointing the hose, and it got your feet all wet.

(After a beat, shamefaced.)

They were brand new shoes. You said.

INA. Yes, I remember. You live next door.

MATTIE. With Mr. Puss.

INA. With the cat, yes.

*(Back to **ALTHEA**.)*

And your other friends –

ALTHEA. Connie and Leif Morrell.

INA. I don't believe Althea's ever mentioned the two of you.

LEIF. *(To **INA**.)* We just met your sister last night. We decided to help her work this mother-of-all-jigsaw-puzzles, and then on our way out, we plan to rob her blind.

*(**INA**'s eyes bug out in surprise.)*

CONNIE. My husband is kidding.

ALTHEA. *(To **INA**.)* Leif and Connie are thinking about buying the house.

INA. I see.

LEIF. It's a beautiful house. We haven't gone over it with the proverbial fine-tooth comb, but we like what we've seen so far. We do understand, however, that the hot water heater may need to be replaced. Are you about to take Althea away or could you perhaps come back around three, maybe four o'clock to do the dirty deed?

INA. Dirty deed?

LEIF. Her official incarceration.

> (*Now* **ALTHEA**'s *eyes widen.* **CONNIE** *is also taken aback by* **LEIF**'s *sudden truculence.*)

CONNIE. Leif, let's go upstairs. I want to talk to you about the house.

LEIF. We aren't gonna talk about the house. We're gonna talk about the fact that I have this sudden, overwhelming need to keep Althea from moving in with her sister.

CONNIE. *Leif!*

ALTHEA. Leif, dear—I appre –

MATTIE. (*Caught up in the moment; a chant.*) Hell no! She won't go! Hell no! She won't go!

ALTHEA. (*Overlapping.*) Mattie, *please!*

INA. (*To* **ALTHEA**, *indicating* **LEIF**.) You just met this man last night?

ALTHEA. Yes.

INA. I don't understand.

ALTHEA. Leif and I decided that we would work this puzzle together.

> (*Indicating* **MATTIE** *and* **CONNIE**.)

Later we got reinforcements.

INA. I understand *that*. What I *don't* understand –

CONNIE. *(Interrupting* **INA.***)* My husband is tired. We're all tired. We haven't slept. Leif isn't usually so rude.

LEIF. Connie's right. I'm usually fairly well-behaved. A regular Boy Scout. I help senior citizens cross the street. I also like to help them finish their damned jigsaw puzzles before they get dragged away to the Land of *No Jigsaw Puzzles*!

INA. First of all, young man, I'm not *dragging* Althea anywhere. She and I have come to what I thought was an amicable arrangement – her moving in with me – if it's any of your business – forgive *my* rudeness, but I didn't –

(*Turning to* **ALTHEA.***)*

Althea, I just didn't expect to find such a – a *circus* here. And I thought you *wanted* to move in with me. Have you changed your mind?

ALTHEA. I – no. It's what I – I know it's for the best.

INA. *(To the others.)* No doubt, she's told you very little of her medical problems. Althea cannot keep living alone. Neither of us wishes to see her go into extended care. Well, at least not yet. It's only right with all the room I have –

MATTIE. You're putting her in the sewing room.

INA. *(An angry outburst.) There is nothing wrong with my sewing room!*

(*To* **ALTHEA.***)*

Why do I have to defend myself to these people?

(*She takes a deep, steadying breath.)*

Althea, you *cannot* finish the puzzle. The moving truck is coming in three hours. You have too much to do between now and then. We both do. That's why I begged out of my lunch date and came here early. I thought you could use the help.

ALTHEA. I appreciate your coming early. Yes, there are a few little things –

MATTIE. Althea, are we going to stop working the puzzle?

INA. *(Answering for* ALTHEA.*)* Yes, you're all going to stop working this puzzle.

MATTIE. *(Remonstrating.)* We worked on it all night.

INA. It's a very large puzzle. How did you ever think you could finish it?

LEIF. We think outside the box, lady. We take the puzzle out of the box and stay outside the box.

CONNIE. Leif, honey, shut up.

LEIF. I always make every effort to complete what I start.

CONNIE. Leif, please.

LEIF. *(To* CONNIE.*)* Do you want the house?

CONNIE. The house.

LEIF. Yes. Do you like the house? Should we buy the house?

CONNIE. I'm – Yes. I do, Leif. I do like it.

LEIF. Good.

(An official announcement.)

We're buying the house.

INA. What?

ALTHEA. *(To* LEIF.*)* You don't want to think it through, dear? None of us is thinking very clearly right now.

LEIF. I love the house. Connie loves the house. Especially the bay window. *And* this basement rec room. I don't mind the lack of sun. You make your own sun in a room like this. We're buying the house. *And* this ping pong table. *And* the puzzle that sits on top of it. And I, for one, plan to keep working on the puzzle that sits on top of it for as long as it takes me to finish it.

ALTHEA. *(To* **CONNIE.***)* Is Leif – is he serious?

CONNIE. He *has* had all night to think about it. I have too.

MATTIE. *(Exultant.)* We're going to be neighbors!

CONNIE. *(Smiling.)* We are, aren't we? Leif?

LEIF. Yes?

CONNIE. Leif?

LEIF. What is it, pumpkin? Say it.

CONNIE. Do you know what I'm going to say?

LEIF. *(Smiling.)* I *think* I know what you're gonna say.

CONNIE. And what I'm going to say – it's something you –?

LEIF. *(Nodding.)* Yes. It's something I.

(**CONNIE** *turns to* **ALTHEA.***)*

CONNIE. *(Significantly.)* Althea, we want you to stay.

ALTHEA. *Stay*?

LEIF. Yes, we'd like to replace the hot water heater but keep the old lady.

ALTHEA. What on earth are you children talking about?

LEIF. I don't want the sunroom upstairs for my office, Althea. I want *this* room. We want *you* to take the upstairs room.

ALTHEA. *(In shock.)* I still don't –

CONNIE. We can't make it any plainer, Althea. My husband and I want you to live with us.

ALTHEA. But you *don't*, honey. You can't possibly—It's the lack of sleep. It's the intensity of these last few hours. Leif, Connie, dear: I simply could not be a burden to you. Please. Let me be a burden to Ina. We are blood.

CONNIE. I have one sister, Althea. One aunt. Leif has no close relatives at all. There is a gap in *our* lives, Althea. We are Swiss cheese too.

INA. *(To* **ALTHEA.***)* This is insanity! You don't even *know* these people!

MATTIE. Yes, she does.

(Slowly, deliberately, wisely.)

She knows that Leif's favorite color is blue. Which isn't khaki. And that Connie's is lemon yellow. She knows that Connie's favorite Katharine Hepburn movie is *Bringing Up Baby*. Leif's is *Pat and Mike*. She knows that Leif has a twin brother in Heaven who he thinks about every day. And that Connie once met Annette Bening in the ladies' room in the Marriot Hotel. They talked about liquid soap. She knows that Leif has a misplaced nipple. And that Connie would make a wonderful mother. And that Leif likes chocolate. And Connie likes strawberry. And most important of all: they both like Althea. There's only one thing she doesn't know, and I'm going to tell you: if you were to add Leif's age and Connie's age together, the square root of that number would be eight. Which is a *very* good square root to have. These are the things you learn when you spend a long night in Venice. And look: the pigeons have taken wing, see?

(She snaps a piece in place.)

CONNIE. *(Staring deeply into the puzzle.)* Yes, I see.

ALTHEA. *(As well.)* I see them too.

LEIF. *(As well.)* That isn't *all* of them, is it?

MATTIE. There are others.

(*Pointing.*)

Here and *here.*

ALTHEA. (*Excitedly.*) Let's put them in the sky. Ina, dear, we've got to put the pigeons in the sky.

INA. (*To* ALTHEA, *stunned, emotionally stung.*) You aren't coming to live with me?

ALTHEA. How can I? I'm needed here.

INA. Just like that? The decision's made?

ALTHEA. The decision is made.

INA. I fixed up the sewing room for you. I bought very pretty lace curtains.

ALTHEA. That was very considerate of you, Ina. And your offer to set aside part of your garden for my sweet peas and tomatoes – that also very thoughtful. But my life has taken a sudden, most interesting turn. *All* of our lives. And we must make the necessary adjustments.

(*Beat, then almost confidentially.*)

And isn't it better this way?

(INA *doesn't answer. This big thing that has just happened has apparently left her confused, clearly dazed.*)

Ina?

INA. (*Her gaze dropping to the puzzle.*) There's a pigeon.

MATTIE. Where?

INA. Right next to Connie's hand.

CONNIE. Yes, I've got it.

(As everyone returns to working the puzzle,
INA *is now drawn in.)*

INA. Herbert and I –

ALTHEA. Yes?

INA. We went to Venice.

ALTHEA. Yes, I remember.

INA. We had such a lovely time.

ALTHEA. *(Tenderly.)* I remember how much you enjoyed
that trip.

INA. *(To **ALTHEA**.)* One of us should call the movers.

ALTHEA. *(Focused on the puzzle.)* In a minute. Work that
little row of rickety houses there.

INA. Where?

LEIF. Right there. Along the smaller canal.

INA. Yes, I see.

MATTIE. *(Singing.)* Then the big baboon one night in
June, he married them...

MATTIE & CONNIE. *(Singing together.)* ...and very soon,
they went upon their Venice honeymoon!

(Lights begin a creeping fade-out.)

INA. *(To **CONNIE**.)* What was she wearing?

CONNIE. Who?

INA. Annette Bening.

CONNIE. A very dramatic black evening gown. It had a
sweetheart neck and feathering at the bottom.

*(**INA** wipes a puzzle piece on her blouse.)*

INA. This one's sticky.

LEIF. I left out Buckminster Fuller. And Sir Isaac Newton. A dinner of true intellectuals. We'll bar Gilligan at the door.

ALTHEA. You didn't tell us your menu.

LEIF. Hold your horses. I'll get to the menu.

(Lights are now out.)

End of Play

www.ingramcontent.com/pod-product-compliance
Lightning Source LLC
Chambersburg PA
CBHW070349120726
47909CB00008B/2781